Robin knew ex[...] prove herself!

She inched one knee onto the red upholstered seat, close to the stranger's jean-clad thigh, never breaking eye contact. Pressing her torso forward, Robin pulled the rubber band out of her ponytail, then ruffled her fingers through her hair.

His cool blue eyes flickered with hot flames. She had his full attention.

In a rush of movement, Robin leaned down and planted her lips onto his. At his moan, she pressed her mouth harder against his and gripped his chin to hold him in place. The muscles in his jaw bunched, then loosened under her massaging fingertips. Good, she was taming the wild beast...who now was moulding his lips to hers, teasing the underside of her top lip with his tongue. He was kissing her back!

Something exploded between them. The next thing she knew, she was almost on top of the man. Fiery sensations rocketed through Robin's body and she suddenly wanted much more...

Dear Reader,

Don't we all have that fantasy guy from our past who once rocked our world? And don't we sometimes secretly wonder what would happen if he strolled back into our lives again?

That's what happens in *Tongue-Tied* when Johnny Dayton, the hometown bad boy, appears years later in Robin Lee's life. Only Robin doesn't realise it's Johnny until after she's darn near hijacked the guy with a mind-melding kiss on top of a late-night-diner table!

How she handles this hot surprise, and better yet, how Johnny handles Robin, made this a fun, sexy book to write.

I love to hear from readers. You can tell me how you liked *Tongue-Tied* by contacting me through www.colleencollins.net or writing to me at PO Box 12159, Denver, Colorado 80212, USA.

Happy reading!

Best wishes,

Colleen

TONGUE-TIED

by

Colleen Collins

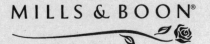

MILLS & BOON®

To Matt, for being my rock.

To my nephews, Sean and Robbie, for being a well
of laughter and love.

And to the memory of my father, Dale Collins, for
being a role model of integrity and grace.

*First published in Great Britain 2003
by Harlequin Mills & Boon Limited,
Eton House, 18-24 Paradise Road, Richmond, Surrey TW9 1SR*

© Colleen Collins 2002

ISBN 0 263 83566 9

21-0803

*Printed and bound in Spain
by Litografía Rosés S.A., Barcelona*

1

"Yo, HOT STUFF, it's almost closing time. Grab some java, make the rounds, and pick up the tab at table two." Al, the short-order cook, barked the orders without looking up as he industriously scraped the metal spatula across the grill. The air smelled of grease and onions, lingering reminders of the dozens of meals Al had fried and grilled that evening at Davey's Diner.

Robin Lee stopped wiping down the wooden butcher block in the back of the kitchen, a chore that was part of her nightly clean-up ritual, and stared at Al. For the four months she'd known him since starting her tenure as kitchen prep at this Denver eatery, he'd reminded her of a Santa Claus gone bad—rotund, gruff and moody. If words were gifts, he gave out few. And of those few, she never thought she'd hear him call *her* something sassy like "hot stuff." Not quiet, industrious Robin who Al had never seen in anything other than one of her four white rayon, wash-and-wear outfits. Add her white sneakers, fine blond hair pulled back into a ponytail, and a slash of pink lipstick that sufficed for makeup and she was hardly the image of a "hot stuff."

Al typically said it like it was, and truth was a trait

she admired above all others. So she chalked up his endearment as an attempt at charm. And he *definitely* needed to slather on plenty of charm—even more slathering than he did with the butter he smeared on everything—if he wanted *her* to play *waitress*.

"Move it, hot stuff," he repeated. "With Dottie gone, I need you out dere."

Charm mystery solved. After Al's fight tonight with Dottie, the fifty-something waitress who'd stomped out of the diner while mumbling a few choice words about control-freak cooks, he was obviously trying to butter up Robin by calling her "hot stuff." He needed her to finish Dottie's few tables so they could close. What Al didn't realize was that no matter how many terms of endearment he concocted, no way was she going "out dere." In fact, she wished desperately she'd never come "out here" to Denver because she'd never been comfortable in the big city. An uncomfortableness that bordered on unbearable after what had happened today.

Tonight of all nights, she wanted to keep to herself, do her kitchen thing and not get involved in potential conversations with anyone, especially total strangers slugging down the remnants of their coffee at midnight in a diner. No way, no how. Not after the worst day in the life of twenty-six-year-old Robin Lee.

Okay—just in case she was being overly dramatic, which her mom often accused her of—if this hadn't been the *worst* day in her life, it ranked in the top five, hands down. As she rinsed the rag she used to clean the butcher block, she mentally calculated, for the umpteenth time, everything that had gone wrong. First, her lifeline to the world—her beloved ten-year-old Jeep she'd nicknamed "Em" for Emily Dickinson, her favorite poet—had been towed because she'd parked on the street-cleaning side of the street. Then she'd spent fifteen precious dollars taking a taxi to DU, Denver University, only to tear into the lecture hall twenty minutes late. But what absolutely skyrocketed today into the top five had been when the professor, who loved to lecture tardy students on the principles of punctuality, decided to make an example out of Robin.

She cringed, reliving the horror of it all. She'd barely sat down before Professor Geller called her to the front of the room and instructed her to tell the class about the key points of last night's homework assignment. She'd read the homework, a novel by Sherwood Anderson, which had been far more than an "assignment"—it had been a privilege because she *loved* literature. She wanted desperately to earn a literature degree because her goal was to one day be a book reviewer—a lofty goal, but one that got her through life's ups and downs. Got her through being older than the rest of the students—something she didn't regret because she'd wanted to stay home and take care of her mom after the accident—got her through being the painfully quiet girl dressed in funky secondhand clothes.

And, she hoped, it would also get her through this hideous moment, being called upon to speak in front of an auditorium filled with snickering students. She *needed* this class for her English lit major. After quickly mulling over her options, she decided her best tactic was to approach the professor and whisper her car-towing story, then try to explain that speaking in front of that auditorium would be an extremely painful experience for not only her, but everyone in that room.

But she'd barely whispered the word *tow* to him when he stepped back and pointed to the podium. Worse, he upped the stakes. In a loud voice, he informed Robin that if she didn't speak, he'd knock her grade down a notch.

She had no choice—she took the challenge. This will soon be over, she reminded herself. In her mind, she assimilated a few facts about one of Anderson's characters and how the author used a small-town spinster to poignantly expose the protagonist's true nature—then Robin would sit down and never, never be late to class again.

She stepped up to the podium, took a deep breath, and leaned toward the microphone. "Sherwood A-A-A..." The vowel stuck, its relentless repetition making a prolonged, strangled sound that reverberated hideously throughout the room. A sea of eyes looked at her with pity and horror while she just kept stuttering, stuttering...hopelessly tongue-tied.

She glanced back at the professor. His bushy white eyebrows were pressed together, as though intellectually analyzing how to handle this situation. *Jerk.* At that moment, in a jolt of gut-deep understanding, Robin realized professors might have the intellect to influence human thinking, but not the common sense to enforce human civility.

Clamping shut her mouth, she scrambled away from the podium, tripping and catching herself as she ran down the steps off the stage. She speed walked up the aisle—avoiding the sea of pitying eyes—made a beeline for the exit and shoved open the doors, gulping lung-fuls of fresh, cool September air.

Then she kept walking.

She pumped her arms and let her feet smash the dry autumn leaves. *Let them crack, crush into nothingness. Just like my dreams.* Because she might as well face it now than later...in a week she was supposed to give an oral report to her psychology class, then there were those "open questions" in her composition class where the professor randomly called on students to verbally re-spond, plus she had no doubt Professor Geller would make an example of her again if she were tardy...so why put up with it any longer? Why not just admit she'd never make it through?

Fortified with that brutal awareness, she'd headed straight for the administration office and dropped out of school. Because no way, no how, was she ever going to face the humiliation of speaking—or trying to—in public again.

"Hot stuff, when I said 'move it,' I didn't mean just your little pinkie!" Al jabbed a fat thumb at the coffee-pot. "Finish serving the tables."

Al's barked command punctured this morning's painful memories. She'd lost enough today—she couldn't risk losing this job, too. Robin glanced over the grill into the dining room. There were only two occupied booths, one by a couple and the other by a guy. She squinted. Funny, for a moment he looked like Johnny Dayton, the megahunk from her small Colorado hometown of Buena Vista. Johnny had been her older brother's pal, the tough kid from the "terrace"—the county-subsidized apartments for the poor. But everything else about Johnny had been rich—from his dark good looks to his smooth-as-velvet charm. Robin had been six years younger and utterly besotted every time Johnny came over to visit.

"Let's mo-o-ve it!"

Al had missed his calling as a prison guard. Taking a deep breath, Robin yanked off her stained apron, grabbed the slick plastic handle of an almost-full coffeepot off the burner and headed into the dining area with the stoicism of a death-row convict. *Soon this will be over. Soon this will be over.* Her tennis shoes squeaked as she crossed the cracked linoleum floor. Approaching the booth with the couple, she watched them break a lingering kiss to stare at her feet. Damn these sneakers anyway. When the couple raised their gazes, Robin held up the pot, indicating did they want more coffee? But instead of responding "yes" or "no thanks" the girl squealed, "It's you! The girl who..."

The girl who stutters. Robin had dealt with people's curiosity, and sometimes their rudeness, all her life. Once, when she'd been ten, and a kid had teased her about stuttering, Robin had blurted out that stuttering made her unique and what was his specialty? When she got angry, really angry, her words could flow effortlessly. But getting red-faced livid wasn't Robin's everyday style. Unfortunately. Because if it was, things would sure be easier.

Robin stared into the heavily made-up eyes of Jill Marcum, the popular student who was in several of Robin's university classes, including Professor Geller's class today where Robin had humiliated herself in front of a gazillion peers. Jill, the girl who always spoke up in class. Jill, the girl who flaunted her great grades the way she flaunted her great body in flamboyant, form-fitting clothes.

But tonight Jill had outdone herself. She'd encased her *Vogue* bod in some sleek leather number that hugged her skin so tight, Robin was amazed the girl could breathe.

Trying not to dwell on her own shapeless white rayon dress, and determined to get this fiasco over with, Robin forced the corners of her lips to curl upward in what she hoped passed for a professional "May I pour your some coffee?" smile. She raised the coffeepot another notch, a silent gesture to back up the "more coffee" smile. Robin was a master at the wordless gestures. Too bad she couldn't find a job as a mime.

"What?" asked Jill, cocking an overplucked eyebrow.

Darn it all anyway. Jill was forcing Robin to talk. She'd failed in front of Professor Geller's class, but she refused to now. Refused to end this day feeling like more of a loser than she already did. Robin sucked in a shaky breath.

"Would you like some more cof-cof-cof..." Her mouth kept moving, stumbling and stuttering over the word, as though somebody else were speaking. These moments were sheer hell—there was nothing Robin could do to stop the stuttering momentum except to clamp shut her mouth, which she did, pressing her lips together so hard they hurt.

In the following silence, Robin realized her feet were shuffling, as though desperate to walk, run, escape this situation, but no way she'd let Jill see her run away *again* from a humiliating situation. As Robin's feet shuffled, her soul shook loose all the feelings she'd managed to suppress—humiliation, hurt, disappointment.

In her fantasy, she'd eloquently say things to Jill that she'd pass on to the other students. How Robin wasn't just some shy, awkward stutterer...how she had dreams and goals...that Robin Lee was more than just a quitter. Instinctively, Robin opened her free hand and extended her fingers wide as though reaching for all the dreams just out of her reach, all the things she wanted out of life....

But the look of pity on Jill's face stopped Robin cold. She'd already faced a sea of such looks today in class, and no way was she going to look at one more.

Closing her free hand into a fist, Robin sloshed some coffee into a cup and turned away in frustration, not wanting Jill to see the pain on Robin's face that said more than a thousand words.

"Poor thing," Jill whispered to her male companion.

Robin headed toward the other booth where the guy sat by himself, not wanting to hear anything else Jill had to say. But Robin would've had to be deaf to not hear Jill whisper loudly, "No wonder Robin never had a boyfriend—after all, what would they talk about?"

Robin squeaked her way to the other booth, wrestling an onslaught of emotions. Just because Robin didn't wear body-molding clothes and shellac her face with makeup didn't mean she didn't have what it took to grab a guy's attention. Heading toward the man sitting solo in his booth, intently reading some papers, she decided to show Jill that Robin Lee, the tongue-tied wonder, had more heat, more va-va-voom than a hundred Jills could ever hope to have. Let Jill tell that to the other students!

To help matters along, Robin undid the top two buttons of her rayon dress. Reaching his table, she leaned over—way over—and heaving a sultry sigh, she aimed the pot to pour coffee into his cup.

"Is that decaf?" he asked absently, not raising his gaze from his papers.

Robin looked at him through the steam rising from the angled pot. Funny, he did sort of look like Johnny...but not really. Johnny had always greeted people with a dazzling smile and a glint in his eye—as a kid, she'd thought he'd absorbed more than his share of sunshine. This guy, on the other hand, had a dark, guarded demeanor, although his brooding, angular looks made her tummy do small flip-flops.

He looked up. "Decaf?" he repeated.

She shrugged, unsure what pot she'd grabbed. She leaned over a little farther, determined to get his mind off decaf and on to a debuttoned view of cleavage.

"Because regular makes me jittery," he continued, his words slowing as his gaze dropped. He puffed out a breath when he caught the glimpse of cleavage. His gaze shot back up, his mouth cocking in a halfway grin that made *her* jittery.

She held the pot midair. Dottie would've probably said, "It's decaf," not caring if it was or not, and left it at that. But Robin was a stickler for the truth and she hadn't the vaguest what she'd just poured. Besides, her hand holding the pot was shaking so hard, if she didn't set this coffee down soon, she was going to slosh this stuff all over the place, getting the guy *really* hot, and not in the way she wanted!

From the corner of her eye, she saw Jill staring at her, mouthing something to her boyfriend. Probably stuff like, "That's the girl who couldn't talk in front of class today—couldn't deal with the pressure and stormed out!" The girl who couldn't, couldn't, couldn't...

Suddenly, Robin wanted to do *one* thing successfully. *One* thing to prove to herself—and nosy Jill—that Robin Lee *could* do something. That she could compete with the best of 'em. Even compete with Jill in the hunky male department! A moment ago, Robin had simply wanted to flash some va-va-voom. Now she wanted to do more...a lot more....

And Robin knew *exactly* what she'd do to prove herself! When Al had called her "hot stuff," he'd been teasing her. Well, she'd show him and Jill just how much "hot" there was in this package of "hot stuff."

She slammed the coffeepot on another table, never taking her eyes off Mr. Decaf. Behind his glasses, his eyes widened. Robin inched one knee onto the red upholstered seat, close to his jean-clad thigh, never breaking eye contact. Pressing her torso forward in the way she'd seen Elizabeth Hurley do in a movie, Robin pulled the rubber band out of her ponytail, then ruffled her fingers through her fine, straight hair. For maximizing boob effect, she took in a lung-bursting breath.

It worked. Those cool blue eyes now flickered with hot flames. The guy looked down, then quickly back up, his glasses sliding slightly down the bridge of his straight-lined, nostril-flared nose.

He frowned. "Uh, do I know you—?"

He was going to blow it for her! If Jill heard him asking Robin who she was, that would ruin everything!

In a rush of movement, Robin leaned down and planted her lips on his to stifle anything else he might blurt. As she held her mouth against his, she fumbled for the table to keep her balance...and slid her fingers into something gooey. Out of the corner of her eye, she realized her fingers had merged with the guy's half-eaten piece of apple pie. Darn it all anyway. She'd have to spring for the pie, and here she was trying to save enough to get her car out of hock. She was debating what to wipe her fingers on when he groaned.

Groaned?

Or maybe he was yelling for help. She pressed her mouth harder against his and, with her non-apple-dipped hand, gripped his chin to hold him in place. The muscles in his jaw bunched, then loosened under her massaging fingertips. Good, she was taming the wild beast....

The wild beast who was molding his lips to hers and teasing the underside of her top lip with his tongue....

Holy cow, this guy was kissing her back! Robin's mind started going into overdrive, panicking that she'd ambush kissed some late-night-diner psycho, but a sane corner of her brain reminded her that she couldn't fail now. Couldn't, couldn't, couldn't. *Relax, keep kissing, let Jill see you being the wildest beastess this side of the Rockies. She'll tell everyone at school and the rumors will shift from dropout Robin to hot-stuff Robin.*

Better check that Jill is still looking.
Robin slid her mouth off the man's, replacing her lips with her apple-gooed fingers in case he tried to say anything. She nuzzled his earlobe while sneaking a peek over his shoulder. Jill was sitting ramrod straight, staring at them, openmouthed.

Yes! Robin, the Love Goddess, rules!

"Oooo!" Robin squealed, feeling warm, wet lips suck her fingers. Shocked, she reared back and watched as the stranger damn near consumed her hand. His mouth was wet and hot and about the best sensation she ever experienced in her whole life. Heat skittered down her fingers, flowed down her arm, building in intensity until it flooded to the pit of her stomach where it flamed like liquid fire. And when he raised his head and cocked her a "you like it, don't you" look, she thought she would combust right there.

She leaned forward and removed her fingers, slowly. She opened her mouth to say something, maybe "Thanks for playing along"—after all, she'd given enough of a hottie show for Jill to fuel rumors for at least a year, maybe a decade—but when Robin parted her lips to talk, words escaped her. In fact, all she was able to do was hunker over him, panting...

"Oh, baby," he murmured in a rugged, husky voice that turned up her inner temperature about a thousand degrees.

Something exploded between them. Later Robin tried to remember exactly what happened...either he tugged her head closer and she went for it, or she went for it all on her own. Whatever happened, next thing she knew, she was damn near on top of the man, sucking face like a woman who'd just landed from a far-away planet inhabited only by females and had just discovered her first, live, hot male.

Robin pawed at his jacket, making small, needy mewing sounds, while in the background she heard small, squeaky sounds—which, in her heat-drenched moment, she vaguely realized were from her feet trying to get traction on the floor. In the failure to do so, she was nearly moon-walking in place, causing the rubber soles of her sneakers to squeak mercilessly against the linoleum floor.

Must...stop...squeaking. Pulling away for a gulp of air,

she shifted her body and hitched one hip onto the table. At this higher position, her breasts were at his eye level, and he clearly enjoyed the view. He raised his hand in a half motion, and in that moment she saw his fingers twitch as though he'd virtually fondled her. Fiery sensations rocketed through Robin's body and she lowered her head, wanting more...

He angled his lips toward hers, and when his tongue again teased the perimeter of her lips, she opened her mouth a bit wider, inviting him inside. Suddenly she didn't care if she mewed or squeaked...didn't care if they were in public...didn't care if two or two zillion people were nearby. All that mattered was this man, his lips, *her needs...*

His hand slid up her waist to a spot just below her breasts, causing her to ache for his touch. With a moan that bordered on a growl, she gripped the soft, buttery leather of his jacket with both hands and pressed herself against him, showing him she wanted his fingers to roam, to feel, to tease her as she'd never been before. Hell, maybe she hadn't spoken up for her car or for her university education, but by damn, Robin Lee, without a single word, was using her body to speak up now!

Her lips found his again and she plunged her tongue into that hot, wet cavern. He tasted delicious. Like sin and heat. Like all those forbidden, lusty bad things a good girl was never supposed to want. Oh, God, she wanted all those things...wanted to experience more, more, more...

"Hold still, honey," whispered the man. "You're about to fall off the table."

"Huh?" Robin fluttered open her eyes and stared into those dangerously blue eyes...had she noticed those thick, black lashes before?

"The table," he whispered again. "You're about to fall off."

She looked down, barely registering that the lower half of her body was nearly *lying* across one end of the table, her feet dangling. Her rayon dress had scooted up to an indecent place somewhere beneath her thigh. She released her death grip on his jacket with one hand and weakly tugged on the hem of her dress.

Strong arms lifted her and set her onto her feet. She felt woozy, weak. When his arms pulled away, she teetered, then fumbled for the edge of the table. Gripping the hard edge, her only concrete link to reality, she looked at the object of her kiss. In their torrid connection, she hadn't really seen the entire man she'd been so focused on his parts—his lips, his eyes, his wonderfully errant hand.... He was one sizzling sight to behold. Rumpled hair—had she done that? Thick lashes that fringed lethal blue eyes—hadn't he been wearing glasses a minute ago? Funny, without them, he almost looked like Johnny again....

She cut a glance to her right—Jill and her boyfriend were gone. Good. Mission accomplished. Releasing her breath in a forced stream, Robin feebly smoothed her dress. Then, she looked back at the handsome stranger with whom she'd become wordlessly intimate.

She licked her lips, wishing she wasn't shaking so badly. "Coff-coffee?" She aimlessly pointed in the general direction of the steaming pot sitting on the other table.

The man's smile kicked up a notch. "Is it as hot as you?" He winked.

Hooo boy. Robin gulped, pushed a strand of hair out of her eyes, and shook her head no.

His grin kicked up a notch. "I've died and gone to heaven," he murmured.

And I've gone with you. Nothing, *nothing* had ever affected her like the last few moments—which could have been hours, days, a small eternity for all she knew. She'd fallen, body and soul, into a time warp of liquid passion where she felt delicious heat, tasted forbidden pleasures... And if she didn't leave at this very moment she'd hurl this damn coffeepot across the room, throw any remaining shreds of decorum out the window, and jump this guy's bones with the fervor of a pent-up, been-without-sex-for-five-years-and-counting woman.

Panting, she stared at him, wondering if he'd read her mind because those sparkling blue eyes of his looked very, very intrigued.

Part of her wanted to suggest they meet again, make a saucy suggestion about getting together for more than a tabletop tryst, be sassy like Dottie or Jill or other hot babes who teased their men with words. But no doubt Robin would start to speak and his look of heated interest would cool before she'd stammered out the first word.

That sobering thought also cooled her overactive libido. Best to leave this situation, now. Leave this guy with the memory of the "mystery waitress" who almost laid more than silverware on his table because he'd never see her again. Even if he came back, she'd be in the back, prepping the kitchen.

With a swivel, she turned, snatched the handle of the pot, and walked stiff-kneed back to the kitchen, the soles of her shoes squeaking relentlessly against the linoleum floor.

As she passed Al, he said with a snort, "I told you to serve *coffee*, not yourself!" With a shake of his head, mumbling something about having thought he'd seen it all, Al continued getting the grill and utensils ready for tomorrow's new day of work.

Robin became super busy doing her own nightly routine, which consisted of turning off the coffeemaker, cleaning the pots, stocking tomorrow's glasses and silverware. Flustered, and still sizzling herself, she fussed and cleaned things she normally left alone—she wiped the outside of the toaster, refolded several kitchen towels, straightened the kitchen rubber mat at least four times. After ten frenetic minutes of hyperactivity, she sneaked a look at the dining room. The stranger's booth was empty....

She tried not to feel disappointed. After all, it was just a crazy kiss, not a date.

But in her heart, she knew it was more than just a crazy kiss. She'd had crazy kisses in high school. Pecks on the lips. Awkward, fumbling kisses. Prolonged make-out kisses that, at best, fired a spark....

This had been different.

This crazy kiss had been a mind-melding, body-bonding, life-altering kiss. Before Robin had walked out onto that floor, she'd known adolescent passion.

Now, she was a woman aching for all the experiences she'd never had. And if she were back home, she'd confess all this to her mother, then refute her mom's suggestions that Robin was once again being overly dramatic. Because, for the first time in her life, Robin had tasted sinful heat—so hot, the rest of her experiences seemed lukewarm if not plain cold.

She glanced at the clock. Twelve-thirty. Going-home time. Robin donned her sweater, the one with colorful kitties crocheted into the threads, for the walk to her nearby apartment. Al was in the back, calling somebody on the pay phone. He glanced up when she waved bye, and although he said good-night in the same gruff voice he always did, he gave her a funny look. Probably a "Try to behave tomorrow night" look. She smiled. She'd have the reputation as a hottie at DU *and* Davey's Diner. Not a bad way to end the worst day of her life.

Walking out the door, the night air had a hint of fall— a teasing cool breeze that traced the late-summer darkness. Above, a full moon hung suspended, like a promise.

"Robin."

A man's voice. She looked down. Not just any man,

that man. The stranger she'd kissed. Her heart leaped in her throat. How'd he know her name?

"You don't remember me."

She looked at him under the streetlight, observed how the light spilled over him in a silver haze. It filtered through his dark, tousled hair, poured over his black leather jacket. Under the light, his face was cast in light and shadows. He looked at her intently, his hands shoved in the pockets of his jeans, his shoulders slouched as he leaned against the lamppost.

Heat shot through her. "Johnny," she whispered.

2

JOHNNY WATCHED Robin stand there, gaping at him. She looked as cute as she had back in grade school. Straight, flyaway blond hair and those big gray-green eyes that took in everything. Those eyes he'd almost recognized back in the diner before he'd been hit with that blast of passion that had melted his logical, rational thoughts... the kind of thoughts that normally filled his mind as Jonathan Dayton, CEO of OpticPower. Which is who he'd been back at that diner, a CEO—well, a CEO in disguise—intently reviewing legal papers for the upcoming board meeting.

Then, like a bolt of lightning, this young, fiery woman damn near burned his logical brain to smoldering ashes.

He looked into her face, trying to read the look in her eyes. If they were inside, under the bright fluorescent lights, he bet he could read what she was thinking right now. He'd been able to do that years ago, back home, anyway. Back then, he guessed her thoughts by the sparkle in her eye—and most of the time, he'd been right. And he'd been able to sense her emotions, too. Hurt darkened her eyes, clouding them over like a distant storm. Joy lightened them to a sparkling green, like sunlight on the sea. A hundred thoughts, emotions would be racing through her, and she'd think keeping her mouth shut meant no one knew.

He knew.

But back then, it was easier to stay focused on her eyes. Now it was damn hard.

The gangly legs had turned shapely. Like the rest of her. She had one of those curvaceous figures that reminded him of early twentieth-century illustrations by Charles Gibson where women were round and pink and womanly. Back in the diner, he'd liked how she felt, how her body pressed against his. Liked even better how she kissed.

He still wasn't certain at what moment he'd been fully aware this hot encounter was with the Robin Lee he'd known. Maybe when he'd caught a determined glint in her eyes, and he'd flashed on a similar look in a girl's eyes back home....

But those thoughts had melted when the kissing heated up. And what a kiss. Hot, intense, full of surprises. One moment she was nibbling and suckling his lip, the next she was doing that squeaking thing with her feet as though one part of her body had decided to dance while the rest of her made love to him. And he'd gone along, at first a bit stunned, then warming up until he was gorging on the sensations, like a starved man sitting down to a feast. An indulgence he never experienced in his logical, business-centered life.

Then afterward, when they'd disentangled themselves, and she stumbled over the word "coffee," the pieces of her personality fell together. Had to be Robin Lee, the kid sister of his childhood pal. But just now, when she'd whispered his name—a soft, awe-filled "Johnny"—*that's* when he knew for certain. He'd heard that same awe-inspired tone from her as a girl. He'd thought it was endearing back then. Now it was downright intoxicating.

Curious as to what lay behind her unique assertiveness-training techniques, he'd hung outside, waiting for her to leave. But now, he realized he'd waited outside for another reason. Knowing it was Robin was like reacquainting himself with his past, a time when life was purer. Not necessarily easier, but *purer.* Less complicated, more understandable. The life he often wished he could step back into again, even while knowing it was too late.

"I—I'm sorry," Robin whispered.

He paused. "Because you kissed me?" He'd leave out the pie-dipped fingers and the writhing on the table.

She nodded.

He waited. Although it appeared she was bursting to speak, she remained silent. He knew she could be chatty as all get-out—he'd seen it many times with her family. But outside her home she clammed up. If only there was more light, he could read the thoughts and emotions in her expressive eyes.

"I don't regret you kissing me," he said gently. He could have said more. Confessed that no woman had kissed him the way Robin had tonight—a kiss tendered with the years of a heart-struck kid turned woman. A kiss that tasted like something sweet turned mouthwatering delectable. And he thought he'd experienced every possible kiss available. Especially after Denver's slick *5280* magazine had nominated him one of the top ten "Most Eligible Bachelors of the Year" two years running, Johnny had had his share of lip-locks. He could almost categorize them. There were the "Good night, will I see you again?" kisses, the "I promise you a good time" kisses, even the "I want to get married" kisses.

But none compared to being blindsided by Robin's sizzlingly sweet, hitched-up-on-the-table, I'm-gonna-take-you kiss. Hell, she was a category unto herself.

But it didn't take an idiot to see that this thunderstruck woman was obviously chastising herself for her spontaneous whatever-it-was moment back there in the diner. She'd surprised him, but he was a master at playing people and situations—and this one he'd play with a sense of humor. Get her to lighten up a little.

"You always serve customers like that?" he teased.

She shook her head rapidly back and forth. A wisp of her blond hair fell across her eye, which she shakily brushed back.

Okay, cool it with the lightening-up approach. Robin Lee had been a stutterer, and from what little she'd said to him tonight, she still struggled with talking.

But damn talented with words. The written ones, anyway. It was as though all that creativity flowed from her soul down to her fingertips as she wrote her essays and short stories. And for one of those she'd won a prize at school. He remembered the day well—she'd been twelve, he eighteen. Johnny had cut classes to hunt for his kid brother Frankie who was fast believing that the solution to poverty was to shoplift and hot-wire cars.

Only instead of finding Frankie, Johnny had found Robin dawdling in a park. It had taken some coaxing, but she'd finally admitted she was playing hooky so she wouldn't have to accept a writing award. After Johnny bought her a chocolate shake at a local pharmacy, she admitted she desperately wanted the award, but she didn't want to accept it in front of an auditorium filled with people because she'd have to say something—and what if she stuttered?

So Johnny had made a pact with her. He'd be there, front row, and all she had to do was look at him and say "thank you" into the microphone. And that afternoon, he'd shown up as promised, and watched as a proud and happy Robin stepped up to the podium, accepted the plaque and while leaning into the microphone and looking directly into his eyes, whispered, "Thank you."

All these years later, he felt as though she were looking at him again with that mix of shyness and steely determination. Only this time instead of the child, he was returning the gaze of a woman.

Shifting his stance, more to hide his body's obvious reaction to her, he checked out the parking lot. It was empty except for a dilapidated green pickup with a broken driver's-side mirror. "I'll see you to your truck."

She shook her head. "I—I'm walking."

He looked up and down the street. Except for a bar a block away, this diner was the sole business with its lights still on. The other buildings were apartment complexes, duplexes, an occasional one-story home. And all had bars on their windows and doors. "Walking in this area of town, at this hour? Are you crazy?"

They stared at each other for a long moment, broken by an apologetic, pixielike smile that finally broke on Robin's face. She shrugged and nodded in the affirmative. "M-my car's..." She blinked slowly, not wanting to start a conversation. She never knew when she'd stutter, and considering she was stumbling through words already, she'd just stop here.

He gave her such a look of understanding, she smiled in relief. *No words are necessary.*

"Then I'm walking with you. I took the light-rail, so I don't have my car." Whenever he felt burdened or troubled, he liked to try and recapture how it used to be, years ago, when life was simpler.

Plus, tonight he hadn't wanted to stay home because Penny would call and call, just as she did every time she dumped him. Only this time he'd told her she was right, no use in their staying together because he didn't want to tie the knot. But as usual, she hadn't liked his response. Even when he'd explained, *again,* that he wasn't the marrying kind because marriage meant trouble. Like the kind he'd grown up with—an alcoholic father, a delinquent brother and a home filled with the kind of furniture most people threw out.

So rather than answer the phone, and rehash the marriage thing all over again, he'd done what he always did when life crowded him—he returned to his past. Or tried to. He'd left the Jaguar at home and jumped on public transportation, hopping off at some coffee shop or diner where he could blend into the crowd as Johnny Dayton, a person he used to be.

And it'd been years since anyone or anything had re-inforced that person...until tonight. Until Robin had whispered "Johnny." Hearing his old name had felt sweet, but painful. Like a knife plunging into him. Slicing deep, but not finding the man she thought he was.

And yet, *she* believed him to be that man....

He clamped tight his jaw, refusing to admit to Robin he was no longer that man. He'd never tell her how he'd changed, who he'd become.

He raised his eyebrows, realizing she hadn't responded to his question. "Is it all right that I walk you home?" Maybe she had someone waiting for her there, like a boyfriend or husband. An irrational jolt of jealousy shot through him.

"It's all right," she said softly. And in the stray light from the diner's windows, he caught her blushing. A reaction so innocent, it nearly knocked him off his feet. Penny never blushed. For that matter, none of the women he'd dated these past number of years had blushed. They'd seen too much, knew too much....

Which made Robin all the more rare.

He turned slightly and said, "Okay, let's go. You lead..." he looked over his shoulder "...which I *know* you can do."

The first block they walked in silence. Johnny was aware of the moonlight-glazed world, the congestion of parked cars along the narrow streets, the late-summer scents of roses and lavender...but mostly he was aware of Robin walking next to him, seemingly lost in her thoughts. For a woman who'd damn near attacked him in public, she was certainly acting shy now that they had some privacy. Not such a surprise, though, when he thought back to the girl who was expressive inside her home, but withdrawn outside.

He slowed his pace, almost imperceptibly, positioning himself slightly behind his walking companion to better observe her. Her head bobbed in time to her determined gait. Her rayon dress swished as she walked, and his imagination wandered, wondering what lay beneath that sound. In his mind's eye, he again envisioned the kind of curves reminiscent of those early-twentieth-century paintings where a woman was soft, rounded... where flesh was alabaster and pink. He'd always had a keen interest in that era—maybe it was the businessman in him, intrigued with the revolutionary changes brought by electricity and the automobile. And as a man, he'd been just as intrigued with what he viewed as the last romantic woman—the Gibson Girl with her long hair curled in a luscious heap on her head, the long lacy feminine clothes, the petal-pink lips curved in secretive smiles....

He stared at the long wisps of Robin's hair and wondered how those glossy locks would look curled on top of her head. He imagined one escaped ringlet falling seductively down her pale neck. She was the type of woman who'd be a lady on the outside, but not such a lady in the bedroom....

He nearly ran into Robin when she stopped abruptly. In the moonlight, he could barely make out her facial features, much less decipher the look on her face, but she was definitely staring at him. Intensely.

"Something wrong?" he finally asked, wondering in some kind of insane way if she'd been reading *his* thoughts. He, who always felt he had the upper hand with people, suddenly felt awkward, as though his mind had been caught in the hot cookie jar.

Silence. More staring. Nearby, a dog barked.

A light breeze lifted a lock of her hair, the moonlight playing wicked tricks as it glinted silver off the blond strands. Impossible to see her eyes, which were in shadow, so he couldn't translate the dead-on stare she was giving him. Years ago, a younger Robin Lee hadn't had such difficulty speaking to him. Maybe she just needed time to feel comfortable with him again.

Or maybe there was something she wanted to tell him. He'd heard from a buddy that there'd been a car accident several years ago in Buena Vista, one involving Robin and her mother, but Johnny hadn't heard much more. Besides, Robin seemed fine....

So why had she stopped? He looked over his shoulder at a square building with layers of windows. "Is... that your building?"

She shook her head no, then turned and kept walking

down the sidewalk. He kept up with her, wondering how long they'd continue on this silent journey.

Robin bit her bottom lip, mentally beating herself up for being the most boring walking companion in Denver, if not the entire world. How many times as a kid had she fantasized about being with Johnny, being able to be the one and only girl in his world, and finally she gets that chance and how does she act? Like some kind of robot. *Silent* robot. Okay, maybe she couldn't compete with women who teased with words, but surely she could do more than march along beside him! She had wanted to confess as much a moment ago when she'd stopped in the middle of the sidewalk and stared at him...but words had failed her.

Even when he'd asked her a question. But rather than *try* to explain what was going on inside of her, she'd just continued walking.

The only redeeming factor to this embarrassing stroll was that her shoes weren't squeaking on the cement.

Finally, they reached her building. She turned, quickly walked up a narrow cement path, and headed up the stairs to her second-story apartment. Behind her she heard his steps following. And with each step, her heart thundered, her breath heaved. Maybe verbally she wasn't speaking to him, but if only he could hear her body! It pulsed and throbbed and vibrated like some kind of human Geiger counter.

On the second-level landing, she turned right and headed down the dimly lit hallway toward a wooden door with the tarnished silver letters *2B*. She'd been in

Denver a year, but this was the first time she'd brought anybody to her place, and here she was bringing *Johnny Dayton* home.

A crazy quote flitted through her mind. "To be or not to be." Now was the moment to be or not to be. Stopping, she fumbled in her sweater pocket for the keys.

Johnny stopped, but not too near. He looked so darned confused, she felt a twinge of remorse. She didn't mean to run hot and cold—it's just when it came to words, she didn't always trust herself. But he had to know that about her. How many times had the teen-aged Johnny Dayton hung out at their house, swigging pops with her older brother, talking about school, cars, girls...and Robin had dawdled nearby, occasionally chiming in when the mood struck. Within the comfort of her home, she had always felt more comfortable opening up, talking....

But then Johnny knew that, too. That day he'd found her hiding out in the park, afraid to go to school because she didn't want to make a speech, she'd told him why. And he'd encouraged her, told him he'd be there, and because of him she had one of the greatest memories of her life—the day she won the middle-school first-place prize for her short story.

Looking at Johnny all these years later, she wanted to pour out everything in her heart. Tell him how he was her first and only crush, how no man compared to the incomparable Johnny...how he stood for everything she admired in the world—truth, integrity, guts. Everyone in Buena Vista knew he'd had it tough—a father who spent more time at the local bar than at home, a kid brother who seemed determined to end up in jail.

But despite his home life, Johnny kept his cool. Never let circumstances drag him down—or never let it show, anyway. She quickly glanced up and down, sizing up how far he had come. The worn leather jacket and rumpled good looks were like the old Johnny. But he was different, too. The gold watch on his wrist looked expensive. And the wary look in his eyes was new, too. How she'd like to ask what had happened over the past fourteen years...

...and how she'd like to tell him today had been the worst day of her life. And explain that crazy, hot moment at the diner. She'd tell him how desperately she'd wanted to one-up Jill, end the day as a success instead of as a loser, so Robin had seized the moment, so to speak.

Forget the diner. In a rush of insight, Robin suddenly knew that if she went inside her apartment without seizing *this* moment, without letting Johnny know the feelings and needs that lay within her heart, this day would truly be the very worst in her life.

She'd really be a loser, all the way around.

Blinking, she turned, and looked at him. *I'm not a loser.* She took his large, warm hand and raised it to her lips, which trembled as she pressed a kiss into his palm. His skin was warm, his scent masculine. She let her lips linger, move imperceptibly against his palm as her heart whispered its secrets.

"Robin," he murmured, more astounded by this simple act of affection than the fiery kiss at the diner. And when she looked up, with that beseechingly sweet look on her face, heat spread through his body, as though radiating from her.

"Oh, baby," he murmured, closing the space between them and filling his arms with her. He nuzzled her hair, her cheek, and inhaled her scent. A hint of lavender teased his senses and he thought how it reminded him of her. Bright, fragrant, wild...the real Robin underneath her quiet exterior.

He hugged her close, relishing the feel of her softness against his body. He kissed her forehead, her nose, and inched his lips to her mouth...but didn't kiss her. Instead, he lingered at the corner of those luscious lips—those luscious, petal-pink lips—and savored the puffs of sweet, heated breath against his cheek.

He pulled back and stared into her half-closed eyes. "What do you want, Robin?"

She licked her plump, moist lips.

That did it. A primal need erupted within him and he backed her against the door, clamping his mouth on hers. Earlier he'd felt like a starving man at a feast cut short, and now he made up for it with a savage hunger. He plunged his tongue into her mouth, devouring its flavors.

She eagerly reciprocated, accepting his kiss with a ferocity that made it damn hard for him to keep control. She kissed with the passion he'd tasted back in the diner. Hot, needy. A flower turned inside out, opening herself and her desires fully to him.

He nipped her neck and she groaned. He proceeded farther, tracing her collarbone with his lips, kissing and licking a path along her silky skin. He tasted her sweat, her fragrance... And when he reached the opening of the front of her dress, where every single pearl-size button was demurely fastened, he knew her clothing made a liar out of her. Those fastenings were a front, showing a woman seemingly tight, contained when he knew damn well that underneath this dress was fire and passion. He pulled away, his fingers lingering on the button.

Her gray-green eyes glinted with need as she leaned back, the movement releasing his hold on that single button. For a moment, she simply watched him, her shoulders pressed against the door, her hips thrust forward ever so slightly. Then, slowly, her hand moved up her dress, flat-palmed, sliding over her torso, up between her breasts, until she gently touched the top button which she rolled seductively between her fingers, watching him watching her.

He never thought he'd lose it over a button. But at this moment, he was in such erotic pain, it took all his willpower not to tear that damn rayon number off her.

She undid the button, slowly. Her lips moved, almost imperceptibly, and she whispered something....

He could barely hear through the blood roaring in his ears. He positioned his head close to her mouth, straining to hear her breathy tones.

"More," she whispered. "More..."

"Oh, God, yes." The soft ache in her voice fired his

need. He gently pulled her hand off the button, then lifted her arm and pressed it against the door, pinning it over her head. He fit her other hand into the held one. With his free hand, he took his sweet time undoing the second button...gently pulled back the material to expose her skin.

He sucked in an appreciative breath. Her skin was pink and alabaster, just as he'd imagined. "You're so beautiful," he murmured. He closed his eyes, then opened them. *I shouldn't take it further.*

As though picking up on his thoughts, she arched her back, thrusting her breasts against him. Such a natural, primitive gesture, almost innocent in its desire. And when she moaned his name, softly, he lowered his head and kissed the skin exposed at the opening to her dress. She tasted silky against his tongue. Smelled erotically sweet, like ripened fruit.

With a guttural groan, he undid the third button with his teeth, playing with the hardened button, imaging it to be her taut nipple. Opening the top of her dress wider with his free hand, he slid his tongue over the white lace that skimmed the top of her bra, gliding his lips over the soft mound of one breast, then the other...

A prolonged, scratchy sound fractured the moment.

Robin? Was he hurting her?

Johnny reared back and looked into Robin's surprised expression.

Another scratchy, tormented sound. Accompanied by a heaviness on one of Johnny's feet.

He quickly glanced down at a chubby cat, covered

with more fur than he thought possible, perched on his right foot! The cat looked up, opened its mouth and emitted another long, scratchy me-e-e-e-o-ow.

With a groan, Robin sank down, her body still plastered against Johnny's, and scratched the cat on its head. "Otto, why aren't you inside your own home?"

Johnny held his breath, his body aflame. Robin had spoken, fluently, which moved him. Obviously she knew this furry feline very well—it probably belonged to one of her neighbors. But in the back of Johnny's mind, he had a crazy hope that maybe her fluency was because she felt more comfortable with him.

Robin lifted the rotund cat and cradled it into her arms. Nuzzling its head with her chin, she scratched it behind its ear. The cat closed its eyes in bliss and purred so loud, it sounded like an engine chugging to life. Damn, he knew just how that cat felt right now.

"You can stay with me tonight, you silly thing." Offering a slight smile to Johnny, she pushed open the door and stepped inside. She took a deep breath, her back to Johnny, hugging the cat tightly against her. Now was her moment. *Ask him inside. Let him stay the night, too.*

Damn, she was shaking just thinking about Johnny being inside her home, touching her, kissing her... savoring a night of love...something she'd never done with any man. Romps in the back seat of her hometown boyfriend's car ended after a few hours, so she'd never known what it was like to have a man hold her the entire night. She could only imagine the sensation of her and Johnny's bodies curled around each other, all night long, then watching the next day dawn on their new relationship as lovers.

And what would that relationship be? Maybe he had no intention of spending the night, and she'd wake up alone. Was there a girlfriend in the picture? There was definitely no wedding ring, but Johnny had always been good—no, make that dynamite—with women. Maybe he was playing the field, and she'd be just another woman in his menagerie....

Only when Otto squirmed in her arms, emitting an irritated meow, did Robin realize she was squeezing the poor cat to her chest, holding on to it like a furry life raft.

Instead of worrying, she needed to cut short tonight's visit. She wished she could grab a piece of paper and write, "It's happening too fast...let's take our time, figure out what's going on between us..." But instead she just stood and stared at him, her eyes growing moist with all the pent-up needs and emotions storming within her. Maybe he'd return...but she knew she shouldn't count on it. This was, after all, an unusual reunion.

Johnny stared into her eyes, which glistened with emotions that confused him, and wondered what to do. He, who prided himself on knowing just how to read and play people, especially female people—digressed into an awkward teenager, unsure what his next step should be. Was she taking the cat *and* Johnny inside for the night? He felt a gut-deep yearning like he hadn't ex-

perienced in years as he wished, damn near prayed,
that he got visiting rights, as well.

Robin held the cat close, and for a moment, Johnny
hated that cute, furry creature. So close to Robin's silky,
flower-scented skin, cuddled and cooed over.

Getting what Johnny wanted, bad.

A twittering sound came from somewhere behind
Robin. She looked over her shoulder, then back to
Johnny. "I—I have a bird."

He waited for her to say more, but she didn't. Instead, after a funny little shrug of her shoulders, she
blinked rapidly—yet despite her nervous gestures, he
swore he read that look in her eyes. Swore she wanted
to ask him inside.

"G'night," Robin mouthed and shut the door.

Well, he couldn't have sworn *that* was going to happen.

Johnny remained standing on her doorstep for what
seemed a small eternity, half tempted to meow patheti-
cally like Otto in the hope Robin would reopen the door
and take pity on him.

*Right. I know how to read and play people. I'm standing
outside a woman's apartment in the middle of the night, con-
templating doing animal impersonations so she'll open the
door.* He heaved a lungful of cool air, willing the chilled
air to temper his fierce physical need. Willing himself to
get his head on straight even if his body was out of control. It's sweet Robin Lee, he reminded himself. *Take a
step back, buddy. Take it easy. Get to know her better before
you jump her bones.* Maybe he'd call her over the next

few days. They'd visit. He'd talk to her...well, try to. Ask to see some of her writing. Ask to see pictures of her family.

The sound of a car cruising down the street reminded Johnny about the light-rail. He flicked his wrist, checked the time. The rail had stopped running a good hour ago. He needed to find a taxi or bus so he didn't end up walking all the way back to Cherry Creek. With tremendous effort, he turned and headed down the stairs, remembering how Robin had clutched that poor cat so hard, its eyes were damn near bulging.

Johnny chuckled under his breath, recalling the image. And what had her last words been? "I have a bird." He crammed his hands in his jacket pockets, fighting the urge to laugh out loud. He'd stood on his share of ladies' doorsteps, but never had one of them said *that* before closing the door.

"I have a bird," he whispered under his breath, hunching against the cool evening breezes, relishing a passing scent of lavender. "I want one, too," he murmured. "A Robin."

3

"CHRISTINE SLAYTER to see you, Mr. Dayton."

Johnny sat in his leather swivel desk chair, looking out the floor-to-ceiling windows that offered a panoramic view of lofty Denver skyscrapers against the distant jagged Rockies. He'd just been enjoying the view, taking a moment to savor the world outside work—something he rarely did anymore—and now he had to deal with Christine. It was like he'd been soaring through the clouds and now he'd crash-landed.

He wished to God he'd never made her a vice president—she seemed to think that meant he liked her more then he really did. But, as his advisors kept reminding him, it made good business sense to give her the title—it was an incentive for her to continue delivering projects under budget, with minimal carcasses in her wake. She was like an imperious queen in that sense—when a project faltered, she went hunting, looking for someone to blame. And inevitably, that person met a gory death—which in business parlance meant she fired the poor bastard on the spot. So far, Human Resources and the legal department had found legitimate backing for Christine's infamous firings, but even Johnny knew that Christine couldn't keep going this way. She would calm down with a bigger, better title—or so she'd whispered to him right after the promotion.

He mistrusted words—those spoken in meetings or whispered in his ear. Robin's expressive eyes flashed in his mind—he trusted what he saw there more than any hollow assurances.

His thoughts returned to Christine, who waited outside his door. Despite her overachiever mentality, he regretted approving that damn promotion because ever since then, Christine had let him know repeatedly that she was available for more. Much more.

But he was also personally to blame for that headache. *Never, ever kiss a woman after two martinis.* Women like Christine took such slightly inebriated overtures to mean there was hope. Forget that it happened a full year ago, the result of a long day's work that turned flirtatious after a few drinks...an overture that went from hot to cold within seconds. For Johnny, anyway.

Blowing out a gust of air, he turned his head slightly toward the intercom. "Thanks, Shelia, let her in." Shelia's physical appearance reminded him of that English actress, Judi Dench. Mature, professional and punctual Shelia had organized his work, and often his life, since he founded OpticPower five years ago.

The door opened with a swoosh and in blew Christine, dressed in one of her designer suits—this one so purple, he imagined her as one of the irises in that Van Gogh painting. An iris topped with blond-streaked hair and a too-toothy smile. "Good afternoon, Jonathan."

His butler William called him Mr. Dayton, like most

OpticPower employees. Christine and her peers called him Jonathan. No one had called him "Johnny" in years...until last night. For a moment, he could even hear Robin's voice, soft and full of surprise, when she'd stepped outside the diner and found him waiting.

He watched Christine swagger toward him, a quasi-masculine movement that looked funny on her scrawny frame. She eased herself into one of the leather guest chairs that faced his desk, and slowly sat down. Her face was overpowdered, caking in the lines around her mouth. For a moment, he wondered where those lines came from. Couldn't be from laughing.

Never breaking eye contact, she crossed one leg slowly over the other, a move obviously intended to give him a flash of her black satin garters.

It wasn't that he didn't appreciate the finer attributes of womanhood—or the flash of skin against lace or satin—but being inappropriately manipulated, whether by words or gestures, was one of his hot buttons. Although he hadn't felt manipulated last night when Robin slammed down that coffeepot and zeroed in for a kiss. *That* was a gloriously spontaneous act, full of passion and want....

"You seem...distracted." Christine looked peeved.

"I was...going over some figures in my head." A very luscious, curvy figure. "You wanted this meeting—what's up?"

A look of hurt shadowed Christine's eyes. Straightening in her seat, she said crisply, "It's the Nexus proj-

ect. Teresa sidestepped the end-to-end test and now we
have a noncompliant test process on a critical delivery."

Johnny leaned forward on his desk, hands folded in
front of him. "It's not like Teresa to bend rules—"

"Brad repeatedly put up roadblocks, so she was
forced to create her own test environment."

Sometimes managing managers was like running a
day-care center. Not that he'd ever done that, but he
sure as hell could after being CEO of OpticPower. Teresa was a senior manager, as was Brad, and yet their
ongoing squabbles were hurting a critical project,
which in the long run, could hurt the company. And
Johnny's priority, always, was to protect the company.
"You undoubtedly have a plan." Christine always did.
Slap a long black wig on her, and she could be that car-
toon character Natasha, Boris's manipulative, conniving sidekick.

She leaned forward, planting an elbow next to a
carved wooden mask that sat on Jonathan's desk. He'd
bought it on a trip to Africa several years ago because
he liked its mythological story, how tribes in the Congo
believed it transformed its wearer into the "Wise Protector and Healer."

"Brad's got to go," Christine said, gazing intently
into Johnny's eyes. "He's not a player, he's a problem. I
want to replace him with Scott, who works *seamlessly*
with Teresa. It's the only way we'll get the test situation
resolved and back on track."

A pungent scent, like spicy orchids, assaulted
Johnny's nose. He recognized the French scent, but

most women dabbed it on their skin. Christine must have poured the stuff on. He wondered if she always sloshed on perfume when in the killing mood. "How long before the test can get back on track?"

"A week."

She hadn't even paused to breathe before that quick response. Oh, yeah, Christine had already planned this, down to the last gory detail. He mulled it over for a moment. He had no real data on this situation, but then he wouldn't. He hadn't built this multimillion-dollar business by micromanaging every single management employee—he'd built this monumental success by focusing on the big picture. And by protecting its vested interests and employees. His stomach knotted. If only he'd been half as successful protecting his own family—a family for whom he'd been more the father than his own dad had been.

"I'd like your buy-in," urged Christine.

Of course she did. It gave her license to kill. Johnny had dealt with these power plays before—he'd give his response just the right spin.

"Before you can Brad, talk to him. He's a valuable asset—let's try to make the situation work before losing a key player."

Christine's eyes widened. "I said he's *not* a player, and yet you used that word—" She immediately pursed her lips and Johnny realized where those lines around her mouth came from. "I know what you're doing. You're saying one thing, but thinking something else. And no one can ever figure out what that is because you're—" She pursed her lips again.

"Don't stop now."

She tugged at the lapel on her jacket, and Johnny noticed the new Rolex on her wrist. Probably treated herself to an expensive bauble after the promotion. No way was she going to say the wrong thing, although she'd admitted enough by her overreaction. He scratched his cheek, mainly to hide a smile that threatened to break. *Must be tough being a newly promoted vice president these days.*

She dropped her hand into her lap. "I was going to say," she said, infusing her voice with phony goodwill, "that you're inscrutable, that's all. Actually, that's an admirable trait. We shouldn't be able to read your thoughts. What kind of CEO would that be?"

A stupid CEO. He'd learned long ago that business was like playing cards—best tactic was to always keep a poker face. "You don't like my not immediately agreeing with your plan of action?"

She paused. "What kind of vice president would I be if I liked you saying 'no' to me?" That phony tone again.

"Actually, I don't think you like anybody saying 'no' to you." It was a dig, but she deserved it for flashing that garter. "Please give Teresa's feedback to Brad," Johnny instructed. "After that, if he and Teresa still can't work together, you and I will talk again."

Christine nodded, halfheartedly, and stood. But she didn't move. Instead she stared at the mask on his desk.

"I've never understood why you like that...ornament."

She looked around the room. "Everything else in this room is elegant, sophisticated." Her gaze traveled across the strategically lit gray walls, the charcoal couch under the oil painting with bold slashes of color, his polished oak-and-chestnut desk. Then her gaze returned to the mask, peering at it as though some hideous little creature had crept into this sanctuary.

Johnny leaned forward and said conspiratorially, "When no one's in here, I put it on and dance around the room." The horrified look she gave him was worth the ridiculous comment. He straightened. "On your way out, please ask Shelia if she'd order in lunch. The usual."

Christine was still staring at him as though he might start dancing any moment. Then she turned and walked briskly to the door, but stopped abruptly when she reached it. "Oh, by the way," she said, glancing over her shoulder, "there's a dinner tonight. Len's department is celebrating the release of several products—care to go?"

Len ran the global products division, and Johnny was fully aware they'd hit their release schedule ahead of time, with customer satisfaction high. He'd already ensured every employee in that division got a little extra thank-you in their next paycheck.

But that thank-you didn't extend to being Christine's date. "I have another engagement. Give Len and his team my best."

Christine hesitated, her tiny eyes glinting with the unvoiced question "what engagement?" Despite his determination to maintain an even countenance, Johnny caught himself smiling at the thought of seeing Robin again. Because at this instant he suddenly knew he really did have an engagement, even if the lady didn't know it yet.

And he kept smiling, even as the door clicked shut.

"YO, DOTTIE, grab some java, make the rounds." Al barked the order to the waitress, who stood behind the kitchen sink, sneaking a puff off a cigarette. On the chipped plaster wall behind her hung a red-and-white No Smoking sign.

Dottie blew out a thin stream of blue smoke. "Who died and made *you* boss?"

Al cocked one bushy eyebrow at Dottie. "It's almost quittin' time, and you need to finish your tables." He gave his head a shake, as though he were talking to a petulant child and not a middle-aged waitress. "And put out that cancer stick. You know the rules."

Dottie made a great show of stubbing out her cigarette, then shot a look at Robin. "Did Mr. 'I Run the Show' order you around last night, too?"

"Order her around?" Al snorted loudly. "I had to do more than that! She's been eighty-sixed from serving coffee in the dining room!" He guffawed, then tossed a wink at Robin over his broad shoulder. "But that's between her 'n me." He swerved his gaze to Dottie. "Right now, *you* need to finish your tables."

"I'll finish *you* if you keep this up," Dottie sassed

back, checking her makeup in a small handheld mirror that she kept on a corner of the sink.

"I heard that," said Al.

She set the mirror down. "You were supposed to." Dottie crossed to the coffee machine, grabbed a pot and took her sweet time walking to the dining area—with Al watching her every undulating movement.

Robin wiped her hands on her apron, enjoying the show. Yesterday, after Dottie and Al had argued, Dottie had stormed out with a few choice observations about Al and his kitchen guerilla tactics. Robin thought she'd never see Dottie again and then Dottie had shown up for work today at 5:00 p.m. sharp—not her usual fifteen-or-so minutes late—acting as though nothing had happened.

But Robin would have had to be blind to believe that! *Something* had happened. Dottie wore a new short black skirt, tighter than what she usually wore, and her brassy blond hair was in a new curly 'do that gave her features a softer, sexier look. Robin had wondered what brought about the change in the older, tough-as-nails waitress...and got an inkling to her answer when Al sauntered into work wearing a freshly washed and ironed white shirt, a new pair of chinos and a big grin. Not only were both *on* time, Robin guessed they were starting to *make* time, too.

They still bickered and quibbled over everything, but now the exchanges had a teasing edge. Robin loved it— and also felt a bit envious. To use words that way must be absolutely divine. To verbally play with them, toy with them, seduce with them... Who needed sex shops? Robin glanced over the grill and saw Dottie heading back from the dining room, her red glossy lips smiling suggestively at Al the whole way. Poor guy. He was scraping his spatula across the grill double-time. Robin figured it was best if she left work pronto—that way, the two of them could close up alone.

But as she tossed her apron into the dirty-linen bin and grabbed her sweater for the walk home, Robin felt a pang of nostalgia. Here she was going home alone, the way she did every night. But last night, for a lovely, passionate interlude, she hadn't been solo. She'd been part of a couple, the way Dottie and Al were tonight. The way the whole darn world seemed sometimes. Her mom often told her if she'd just stop shying away from guys, show them that she was interested, she'd have more beaus than Scarlett O'Hara.

What Robin felt her mom never understood was that it wasn't about *shying* away—it was about *speaking* up. But because she was quiet with most people, they took it to mean that she wasn't interested. That's one of the reasons Robin admired Emily Dickinson. From what Robin had read about the famous poet, they were alike—quiet on the outside, passionate inside.

Robin's mind flitted back to last night. Maybe her voice had been quiet, but her body had spoken volumes! And Johnny—the fantasy man of her childhood dreams—had heard every nuance. Words hadn't been necessary. Their bodies had conversed and interacted in a way she never had with any other guy. She touched

the top button of her white rayon dress, remembering
how Johnny had suckled and nibbled that button—for a
heat-drenched moment last night, she'd thought he was
going to rip it off with his bare teeth, then devour her
dress, her slip...

And when his lips reached her bare skin... She
gulped a breath, suddenly finding it difficult to breathe
just thinking what that man's mouth could do on a
body.

"Hon, you okay?" As Dottie walked by, she patted
Robin's arm.

Robin nodded briskly, her cheeks burning. She had to
stop this trip down fantasy lane. One hot encounter
didn't mean she'd see him again. And she wanted *him*
to take the next initiative, not her. Not that she was con-
servative—God knows he wouldn't think that about
her after her tabletop assault last night—but she wanted
him to make the effort to see her again. *If only I'd tried to
say something, maybe how wonderful it had been seeing him.
But, nooo, I just announced I have a bird and shut the door.*

Robin winced. She hadn't even had the wherewithal
to try and explain that with a bird and a cat in the same
apartment, she knew it was going to get chaotic, so it
was best to just call it a night. That would have explained her strange good-night, without going into all
the other reasons—the real reasons—she'd cut it short.

With a wave to Dottie, Robin squeaked her way
across the dining room floor to the door. In the front
window, she flipped the Open sign to Closed, yanked
open the door, and stepped outside, filling her lungs

with fresh, cool night air. Overhead, the moon glowed, bringing back memories of her moonlight stroll with Johnny.

"You're beautiful in moonlight, like Diana, the goddess..."

She looked down. There, where he'd stood last night when she walked outside, was Johnny. Dressed in khaki slacks, topped with that lethal leather jacket, he slouched underneath the streetlamp looking like a bad boy on the prowl. For her?

"Diana?" she whispered, more out of nervousness than a question. She was awestruck to see Johnny standing there, waiting for her. *He took the initiative. He wants to see me again.* "The m-m-moon goddess."

"Yeah." He stepped forward. "The moon goddess."

The man wore leather, macho and myth swirling around him like an aura she could almost see.

"No car again, I see," he motioned toward the parking lot with the sole green pickup. "You never told me the story—is it getting fixed?"

Fingering the button on her dress, Robin tried desperately to assemble the words in his question, but just the nearness of him made her light-headed, giddy. He asked something about her car. Had she gotten it fixed? Maybe, soon, she'd be able to explain she wouldn't have a car until she had one hundred and twenty extra dollars, the cost to spring her automobile from the garage where it'd been towed. Instead, she shook her head no. About six or seven times.

He paused, as though debating whether to say something, then he pushed off the streetlamp and headed toward her. It was the same confident, ballsy walk she remembered from years ago. Back in Buena Vista, a teenage Johnny had acted as though he were ready to take on the world. She shivered at the powerful image, and from her own reignited yearnings. What had she said last night at her door? *More...more...*

And right now, when Robin looked at Johnny, that's what her entire body was saying. *More. More.* She was ready to melt into a hormonal pool right here....

He stopped several feet in front of her, his hands shoved deep into his pants pockets. He cocked his head as though to look at her better, and when he did, a strand of dark hair fell over his brow. "May I walk you home again?"

She swallowed, hard. *Pretend you're Dottie,* she told herself. *Pretend you can speak up, tease a man with your words.*

"Yes!" Robin blurted, a bit more empathically than she'd meant to sound.

Johnny grinned. A wide, satisfied grin that made her heart leap into her throat—if she tried to speak again, it would be impossible. Forget stuttering, she didn't even know if she could *breathe* properly right now. This hunk of hottie acted as though there was nothing better in the world than to escort *her* home. She edged out of the stray streetlight so Johnny wouldn't see the redness flooding her face, so he wouldn't know that his smallest gesture sent shock waves through her world.

She wrapped her sweater tighter around her, mainly

for something to grip, and started walking in the direction of her apartment.

"Hey," Johnny called out. "Wait for me." The slap of his footsteps slowed as he caught up to her. "Is there a fire?" he asked with a laugh.

Hooo boy, that's the understatement of the year. Robin stopped, shook her head no.

He looked at her sweater that she'd damn near double-wrapped herself in. "Did I...upset you?"

"No!" She squeezed shut her eyes, wishing it were possible to teleport her body back in time, oh, five minutes so she could have another chance to act *normal* this evening. "I—I mean yes," she whispered.

"I do?"

She held up her thumb and forefinger, indicating "a little." He kept staring at her with that confused—or was it amused?—look. A hot wave of need swept over her as she looked into those twinkling eyes. No man had a right to look so sexy doing absolutely nothing but standing.

He stepped closer and she caught the familiar scent of his cologne. That killer musky scent was now forever linked to last night's moment of spontaneous booth combustion and later, the moments of body-melding heat against her apartment door. She licked her lips in a useless effort to put back some of the moisture that had left her mouth.

"So, I upset you a little?" he said in that husky, teasing voice that made her skin tingle.

"A lot." The words escaped her lips in a breathy, mewy voice she didn't recognize.

He inched closer. "Mmm. Am I upsetting you as much as I did last night?"

She almost toppled over right there. Damn. Not only was she terrible at speaking, her body was betraying her big time. Shaking. Gulping breaths as though there wasn't enough air left in the world. He had her so excited and befuddled and hot, she didn't know what her body would do next.

She smiled. So broadly, she knew she looked like a fool. Now she'd need to teleport back in time at *least* ten minutes. No, back to another era because she was definitely not making quite the impression she wanted during this particular lifetime.

Johnny scratched his chin and chuckled. "The pie?"

He thought she was smiling like the Cheshire Cat over their booth encounter. No, but now that he brought it up, she thought about how her shoes squeaked against the dining room floor and she giggled.

He raised his eyebrows in a silent question.

She pointed at her tennis shoes.

He looked down, frowned, then laughed out loud—a deep, rich sound that filled her soul with joy. "I've never met a woman who needed traction for a kiss."

They continued laughing together, sharing the memory. After the laughter subsided, she realized she wasn't shaking anymore. She could even breathe normally! She still had butterflies flying madly in her tummy every time she looked at Johnny, but otherwise, her body was behaving. It was nice to be relaxed, unguarded with him.

Johnny reached over and stroked her arm. "I remember you used to laugh a lot when you were a kid. At home, you were a real fireball. And, if you don't mind my saying this, quite a chatterbox at times."

"Yes." At home she'd been comfortable, even if she occasionally stuttered. But she usually felt uncomfortable outside her home—make that times ten in the big city of Denver. So not only did she rarely converse with others these days, she couldn't even remember the last time she'd shared a laugh—something she'd done a lot with her mom and friends back home. This year had been lonely, being a small-town girl in the big city.

He touched her hair, sweeping a loose strand out of her face, although she felt more that he wanted to console her, as though he'd read her thoughts. "It's okay," he whispered. "Be as quiet as you want. I know when you're ready, you'll let your guard down with me." He gently took her elbow and steered her toward the direction of her home.

Robin fell into step alongside Johnny, grateful for his understanding. She felt warm...and comfortable. *Comfortable.* Then she realized how being with Johnny was like having a special part of Buena Vista again. *I can manage now—he's part of home.* Robin slid her hand into his, smiling when he gave her fingers a reassuring squeeze.

As they strolled along, she occasionally glanced up at him, recalling the Johnny from years ago. He'd been gregarious, outgoing and he was always laughing with his friends the way he laughed with her tonight. She frowned. No, back home he laughed *differently.* Back then, he'd been more easygoing, and everything about him—his laughter, his tone of voice, his walk—had been looser, freer. Funny how he'd said someday she'd let her guard down. Looking up at his strong profile, the tight line of his lips, she had the unshakeable sense he, more than she, had his guard up. What had the years done to him? When had Johnny adopted that invisible armor?

She squeezed his hand, just as he'd done a few moments ago, wanting to show him that she cared, that no matter what had happened, she was on his side because just as he knew the old Robin, she knew the old Johnny. That no matter what had forced him to don that armor, she knew his truth.

A half block away, they passed a condo with music wafting from an open window. Closer, Robin recognized an old Frank Sinatra tune, one she remembered from years ago when her dad still lived with them. A memory surfaced. Five-year-old Robin wandering into the living room and seeing her parents dancing slowly, swaying in time to the music, lost in their own world. That's how she wanted to remember her dad—as the man who loved her mom, loved them. Not as the man who deserted the family.

And it's also how she wanted to remember her mom. Dancing, without the limp that was her legacy after the car wreck. Robin bit her bottom lip, fighting a surge of familiar guilt. If her mom were here right now, she'd insist Robin stop that self-recriminating nonsense and remind Robin how "the universe" makes things happen for a reason. Although Robin still questioned how a loving universe could cause another driver to slam into her mother's car. Cause her mother's leg to be shattered.

Cause the other driver to lie, saying he hadn't run the stop sign.

And how the universe could cause Robin—the only passenger in her mom's car and the sole witness on her mother's behalf—to stutter hopelessly at the trial, resulting in her mother losing her lawsuit.

But amazingly enough, despite everything that had happened, her mom never stopped talking about "the universe" as though it were her best pal. Out of respect to her mom, Robin tried not to relive the past or wallow in blame. But it wasn't easy.

The Sinatra tune wove its way through Robin's memories, drawing her back to the present. Music had always been one of Robin's great escapes. She began singing softly, harmonizing with the melody.

Johnny stopped. "I'd almost forgotten you sing," he said quietly. When she paused, he squeezed her hand. "Please. Continue."

She kept singing softly, enjoying the freedom of just letting the words flow. When she sang, she didn't stutter. Johnny joined in, his husky voice mingling with hers, sharing the words, the mood. They continued walking. Even when they'd long lost the music, they continued to sing softly together, all the way to her porch. He couldn't really carry a tune, she noticed, but didn't care. Just his making the effort made her think that maybe his guard was slipping, just a bit.

A few minutes later, they reached her doorstep. Under the hall light, she could again see those devastating blue eyes. That lock of hair had fallen across his brow again, giving him that bad-boy edge she remembered from years ago. Maybe he'd changed, but she could still see the tough kid within the man. See her Johnny...the Johnny she remembered...

Rising on tiptoe, she touched her lips to his. So lightly, it was a hint of a kiss...a hint of a promise...

She settled back onto her feet and looked up into his face.

"What do you want?" he asked huskily.

She eased in a long, calming stream of air. Last night she'd almost invited him inside, but she'd been concerned things were moving too fast. But she didn't feel so concerned about "fast" after that stroll home, their singing to Sinatra. Only one issue remained unresolved...

"Are you—?" She pointed to her ring finger.

"No. There's no one else in my life right now." He cocked one eyebrow in a question. "But you didn't answer *my* question," he teased, looking deeply into her eyes. "What do *you* want?"

She smiled and took her key out of her pocket. Turning, she quickly inserted it into the lock and opened the door. Stepping inside, she turned and boldly reached for his hand. "I want more," she whispered, pulling him inside.

4

JOHNNY DAMN NEAR stumbled inside. He'd had his share of women entice and tease him into their homes, but this was the first time one had boldly announced she wanted *more*—more of *him!*—then grabbed his hand and pulled him inside.

A lesser man would have fallen flat on his face out of hot anticipation.

As his eyes tried to adjust to the shadows, Robin released his hand, closed the door, and headed toward the sole source of light in the room—a decorative desk lamp in the far corner. The base appeared to be a brass figurine with lily-shaped amber fixtures. Its rays gilded nearby walls and furniture with a soft, honeyed haze.

As Robin approached the desk, the lamp glow highlighted the edges of her white dress and flared the tips of her blond hair. Johnny's gaze dropped, observing how the light also teased through a section in the lower half of the dress, offering a provocative outline of her curvy thighs—and the space between—as her body moved. He'd seen his share of teasing, sexy outfits—everything from garters to bustiers to see-through black lace numbers. But at this moment, nothing was as hot, as enticing, as light filtering through a plain white rayon dress.

She stopped next to the desk, fussing with something alongside it. He didn't want to take his eyes off her, but he also wanted to know what else was in the room in case things got out of hand—and he fully intended for things to get out of hand—so they didn't accidentally knock over furniture or fall on something sharply uncomfortable.

First, he checked out the desk, which was covered with an array of objects—books, photos, enough mugs to start a coffeehouse. Stray light fell golden on a patch of hardwood floor below the desk, then faded toward the center of the room, where it lightly glazed a heap of round shapes. He squinted. Pillows? Yes, those heaps were a grouping of pillows. *Interesting.* Did she practice yoga with pillows? Lie there while reading? His groin responded to other ideas with those pillows... He shifted his weight while glancing around the rest of the room, but there wasn't enough light to really see much else.

A loud chirp told him they weren't alone.

"Yes, Mick," whispered Robin, her back still to Johnny. "It's your dinnertime."

Mick? Right. The bird.

Johnny was grappling with the significance of this name—was it an old boyfriend?—when Robin turned and headed back toward him. Again, he watched the light play naughty tricks through the area between her legs, then raised his gaze to her darkened face, framed by that fine blond hair, the tips ablaze with captured light. Her undulating, white-sheathed, gold-tinged image brought to mind a sexy angel. A sexy, titillating angel. Sweetness and heat all rolled into one.

She reached him and stopped. They stood a few feet apart, but with her face in shadows, he could only wonder what message lay in her eyes. Was she ready for him to kiss her? He licked his lips, wanting to sample her again. Imagined his mouth pressed against those petal-soft lips, his tongue tasting, exploring... He leaned forward, but stopped.

Because she hadn't budged. Not even a millimeter. Just stood in place, staring at him. Was she being tentative? Then she raised her hand...and...just as he thought she was going to touch his face, the hand glided straight past his head.

Snap.

The room blazed to light. He blinked, blinded by the ceiling light that assaulted the room with a stark brightness. He realized she'd reached past him to flick the light switch next to the door. Why? Squinting, he looked into Robin's face, but barely had the time to register her flushed cheeks and glistening eyes before she turned and walked away, disappearing down a hallway to their right.

He gave his head a shake. What was *that* about? He felt more stunned, standing alone in this godawful brightness than he had last night when she'd announced she had a bird and shut the door! He pressed his thumb and forefinger against his eyelids, giving himself a few moments for his eyes to adjust. And giving a few moments for himself to reassess this situation.

Point one. You're inside her place, not outside. Two, she hasn't yet announced that she has a bird, which is a good sign. Three, the lady said she wanted more.

He'd stay.

Dropping his hand, he blinked at the room. One thing he believed in business was to never second-guess a decision, so unless she gave him more clues that she'd changed her mind, he'd cool it with the reassessments. Instead, he'd distract himself by checking out Robin's home. He wanted to get to know her better, discover clues about things she liked, things she did in her spare time.

It was a small room, no more than twenty by thirty, with a single passageway to his right. He glanced down it. Rustling sounds intermixed with cabinet doors clicking open and shut emanated from a doorway halfway down the narrow hall. He stepped forward to get a better look into the room and saw the side of a refrigerator. Beyond it, a hanging three-tiered wire basket, apples and bananas in the top basket, onions in the middle, and an assortment of bags filled with foil-wrapped pieces—candy?—in the bottom. *Okay, that's the kitchen and the lady likes to cook...and nibble.*

The last thought made him hot all over again.

Smiling to himself, he craned his neck to check out what other rooms were down that hallway. If things went as he hoped, he wanted to carry Robin to the correct room when it was time for bed...

There was one more door, a little farther down the hall opposite the kitchen. Just inside this second room, he caught a flash of bright colors, which appeared to be bright tropical birds imprinted on a clear plastic shower curtain. The other door was to the bathroom.

So where was the bedroom?

His gaze returned to the room in which he stood, comprised of a small wooden desk, a cage with a green-feathered lovebird, an old yellow recliner that faced the windows against the opposite wall, a bookcase...and a pile of orange, pink and green pillows in the center of the room. Interesting. She bought brightly colored pillowcases, stuffed them with pillows and made them part of her living-room decoration. The lady was very creative. He hadn't seen this many vibrant colors in the same room since he toured the avant-garde exhibit at the Denver Museum of Art last year. Must be hell for her to wear plain old white to work, he mused.

But where was the bedroom? There was one more door, tucked next to the bookcase, which offered a narrow view of a cramped closet.

Was *this* the rest of her apartment? If so, the room he stood in also had to be her bedroom.

A memory socked his insides. He grew up in a place like this—but comparisons stopped there. Whereas Robin's home was brightly decorated and smelled like potpourri and vanilla, his home had looked dingy, smelled musty. His and his brother's beds were sleeping bags in a corner of the living room. Their father, when he was home, slept in another corner of the room on a cot that doubled as their couch during the day. They had a few pieces of other furniture—some metal folding chairs, a scarred and chipped table, a pole lamp—objects they'd either lifted from the town dump or some good Samaritan had given them. They cooked on a hot plate in the bathroom, washing the dirty dishes in the tub. Ever since then, the scent of hand soap always triggered memories of greasy meat and fried potatoes.

The memory assaulted his senses like the sudden light had assaulted his eyesight. Fortunately, at that moment Robin re-entered the room, tugging his thoughts back to the present. Carrying a bottle of water and a bag of seeds, she stopped in front of Johnny, her eyes a sparkling green—made him think of splattered sunlight on the sea. She was obviously happy, but the way she slowly shuffled one foot back and forth said more. Was she embarrassed to have dragged him in here, then bring their passionate ride to a screeching halt so she could feed her bird? He'd never had a woman put a bookmark on passion to take care of a pet—but he liked it. Said a lot about Robin's character.

But that shuffling foot of hers gave away her nervousness.

"It's okay for you to take time to feed..." What had she called her bird? "...Mike."

"Mick," she gently corrected. With a relieved smile, she crossed to the cage. As she approached, the lovebird hopped eagerly along its perch, twittering and chirping excitedly. "Here, Mick, honey," cooed Robin, pouring water from a bottle of Evian into the bird's water dish. Evian? From the looks of her place, he'd have thought she'd just offer her feathery friend tap water...but Evian? Next, she carefully poured some seeds into another bowl, while whispering into the cage and playing with a little bell that hung on one of the outside bars. Man, that bird had it made. Living with a luscious woman whose priority in life was to feed and love him forevermore. Not bad. Not bad at all. Johnny wouldn't mind a piece of that kind of forevermore...

Whoa, buddy. This is the beginning of something... temporary...not the whole shebang. She's got her priorities straight—get yours straight, too. He reminded himself what those were. First, the company. Right up there with the company, its employees. And after that, it's...

Robin turned and looked at Johnny.

*It's...it's...*hell, he didn't know what else mattered in his life except for this moment, this woman. He eased in a long, deep breath, catching a hint of her lavender scent that brought back hot memories from the night before. Memories that shot straight through his logic and ricocheted wildly through his body, igniting other sensual snapshots of last night's encounter—how her skin had tasted under his tongue, how her body had softly molded against his. He reminded himself that this was their first time and he wanted to take it slow, make it memorable, which fought every instinct to just cross the room and bend her over that desk...

She stared at him, a bottle of water in one hand, the seeds in the other. Even from across the room, he could see her full breasts heaving and knew she wanted exactly what he wanted.

"H-hungry?" she whispered.

"Not for seeds."

A rosy blush crept up her neck and filled her cheeks as she looked at what was in her hands, then back at Johnny. "No-o-o," was all she said, giving him a "you're silly" look.

He loved that look. Nobody gave him such looks at work. Nobody dared. He knew she'd been hot to bring him inside, understood she needed to feed dinner to Mick before, uh, feeding the desires of the other animal in the room, but now she was stalling. At least her foot wasn't shuffling. Yet.

"Can I, uh, help you?" He didn't know what the hell he meant. He, the master of spin, was trying to wing it in an awkward moment with his body on fire and his mind on hold. But Robin seemed frozen next to the birdcage, clutching bird food, struggling for words, no doubt.

It was time for Johnny to do something.

He walked over to her and, after gently touching her arm, glanced into the cage at the lovebird happily feasting on seeds.

"So this is Mick," Johnny said, forcing himself to sound conversational.

Robin nodded. A wisp of her blond hair fell across her brow.

Johnny pulled the wayward strand off her face, letting his fingers linger on her warm, moist cheek.

"Named after Mick Jagger?" He meant it to be a joke, something to lighten a heavy moment, but had to force himself to keep a straight face when she nodded again. What woman named a little green-feathered, peachy-faced lovebird after a hard-core rock star? Robin, with her creative imagination, that's who. So, she dug The Stones. Probably other rock bands, too. U2 was coming through town soon—maybe he should get tickets for the two of them.

"Has your love life had many boyfriends...uh, I mean has your lovebird had as many girlfriends as Mick?" He was blowing it. His tongue was misbehaving the way the rest of his body wanted to. "Okay," he said sheepishly, "obviously I'm curious about your love life—" Hell, he wasn't sure what he was asking. He never got this tongue-tied. *Never.* But her signals were throwing him off. If she wasn't in her mid-twenties, he'd swear she was a virgin the way she was suddenly acting, but that couldn't be true. Not in this day and age. And despite the fact that he could benefit greatly from a blast of fire extinguisher right now, he wouldn't ever ask a lady if she was a virgin. Not directly. "You asked me if there was anyone else, so it's only fair I ask, too." He paused. "Is there another man in your life?"

"No."

He waited, but she just stared at him with those green sparkling eyes. "No one waiting for you back in Buena Vista? A former boyfriend?" *Tell me I'm not the first.*

A shadow flitted across her face. "I-it ended."

So he got his answer, but he regretted asking. He

wanted that sparkle back in her eyes. He glanced at Mick, then winked at Robin. "Enough about your past. The real question is, has Mick had as many girlfriends as his namesake?"

She held up her forefinger.

"Oh," Johnny said, as the meaning dawned on him. "He's had one girlfriend."

She nodded.

Mick had probably lost his mate. Two strikes. "Well," Johnny said quietly, "she was lucky to have had him...and you."

An appreciative smile curved Robin's luscious lips.

Change the subject before strike three. He glanced at her desk and the books scattered across it. Two had mind-altering creatures on their covers—one looked like a dragon with wings, the other an ant with human eyes. "So you like fantasy?" He meant it as a comment about her reading preferences, but immediately realized how he wanted to know *her* fantasies, explore what lay beneath that seemingly shy, white-clad facade.

"Yes," she whispered. "Among others."

Among others. Had to mean other types of books. She spoke fluently, which pleased him. She was relaxing with him. He'd keep it casual, continue the conversation, get her to open up more... But first, she had to release her death grip on the water and seeds.

"Want to put those down?" he asked, nodding toward what she held in her hands.

She nodded and quickly placed them on the edge of the desk.

He held out his hand and she gingerly placed hers in it. It was so small, so soft. He wrapped his fingers around hers and looked around the room. "Well, we've discussed your pet, your books... Let's see what else is on this tour."

She giggled. He loved the sound. Infectious, light, with just a touch of sultry. Damn, he was getting a hard-on just listening to her laugh.

Holding her hand, he walked toward the window, a tremendous act of willpower considering the tightness in his pants. Facing this window was the recliner—next to it, a small table littered with pens and several yellow-lined writing pads filled with cursive script. Robin's writing. He wanted to pick up the paper and read the words, see what ideas and thoughts and fantasies filled her mind.

"You're still writing."

"Yes."

He looked up, not wanting to stare at the paper too long. It was an infringement of her secret world. Instead he stared out the window. Below, a single streetlight highlighted a narrow alley. Directly across the way, a block-long brick building with boarded windows. Not a very pleasing view. But obviously, from the placement and angle of the recliner, Robin often sat here, looking out the window.

There were some framed pictures on the far wall, so he headed in that direction, lacing his fingers with hers as they strolled across the room, sidestepping the heap of pillows. He guessed some of those pictures would be of their hometown, which would provide an opportunity for them to view some shared history, maybe even converse if she felt comfortable enough.

The first picture was Robin and her brother, Bud, taken about the time Johnny and Bud were in high school—which brought back an avalanche of memories. Johnny and Bud flooring Bud's old Caddy on a dirt road outside of town, playing football—until Johnny had to quit to take an after-school job—hanging out at Bud's house where there were plenty of laughter and pranks. So unlike his own home life. "I loved visiting your family," he murmured.

Robin responded with a squeeze of his hand.

Johnny moved to the next picture. A recent picture of Robin's family. Her mom's hair had grayed, but he still recognized the gentleness in her eyes. Bud stood behind her. Absently, Johnny raked his hand through his hair as he stared at Bud's receding hairline. And in a chair next to her mother sat Robin, her hair shining gold in the sun, smiling that full-lipped, pixie smile, but something in her eyes seemed...sad.

"When was this picture taken?" he asked. But what he really wanted to know was what had saddened Robin.

"Before...Denver," Robin answered softly. She stared intently into the photo, her expression almost as sad as the one in the picture.

She shifted her gaze to Johnny's. For a moment, they stared into each other's eyes, and Johnny was pained at the shadows he saw there. What had happened before she left Buena Vista? Why was she here, working in a diner of all places?

As though she could read the questions in his eyes, Robin gave a little shrug, then released his hand and headed back down the hallway.

Johnny watched her walk away, listened to the swish of her dress, and decided to leave. Maybe she'd wanted him to come inside, maybe she wanted all the things Johnny wanted tonight, but there were other things on her mind—things he'd seen in that photo. Whatever had happened, it had changed her life dramatically. It wasn't a matter of second-guessing tonight's situation, it was simply his gut telling him to give the lady some room. Give her time to think through their attraction, and figure out what she wanted.

He decided that when she came back into the living room, he'd wish her a good evening and jot down his home number so she could call when she felt ready to get together again. Hell, that wouldn't work—Robin probably hated using the phone. He glanced around. No computer. Couldn't leave his e-mail address, either. Well, he'd ask if she'd like to get together again soon. If she nodded, he'd say he'd call soon, tomorrow, and they'd make plans for dinner.

So caught up was he in his thoughts, he barely noticed a movement—a flash of white and pink—in his peripheral vision. He looked over. His mouth went dry.

Robin stood at the entrance to the hallway, the glow of the hall light suffusing her in a golden haze that tinged her hair like a halo. The sexy angel, again. But most stunning was that she'd stripped down to her shiny white slip—a knee-length, form-hugging garment with lace trim that skimmed the top of her breasts. Her legs were bare, the toes curling as though she were embarrassed or nervous. Her hands were tightly clutched in front of her.

"Robin," he began, then had no idea what to say. What was this, the second or third time tonight he'd been unable to find the right words? He never had this problem. But this woman churned his mind and desires like no one ever had. The only sane thought that surfaced was that he didn't want to be a buffoon with this sweet woman in a dime-store slip, painfully anxious about her sexual boldness.

She sensed his quandary, turned and put a CD on a disc player that sat on the bookcase. Soft piano music filled the room, followed by a female singer's sultry voice crooning a tale of passion and love.

Robin stood, her chest heaving with her breaths. She was so nervous—should he suggest she stop? What had he planned to say? That he'd call, and they'd plan a dinner date—his gaze dropped.

Hot damn, she's not wearing anything underneath that slip.

Her taut nipples strained against the sheer material—so sheer, he saw the seductive curves of her breasts, the dark rose of her nipples. And below, he could see the shadowed patch of curls between her legs.

He looked back up as she raised one trembling hand

and gently pulled down one of the slip straps, exposing a softly round shoulder.

What had he been thinking before? That he'd ask her to stop? Hell, he was unable to stop *himself* from staring at the beautiful vision that stood before him, offering herself to him. Had he ever been the recipient of a more precious gift?

Seeing his reaction, she smiled, then reached over and pulled down the other strap. Her teasing lavender scent threaded the air, like an invisible lasso, reeling him in. If he'd had any lingering thoughts about leaving, they disintegrated when Robin began slowly gyrating her hips in time to the music, seductively rolling and thrusting to the beat of the music.

He'd been trying to take it slow, but to hell with that.

He closed the space between them in two steps and gathered her into his arms, inhaling lungfuls of her scent, burrowing his lips into her silky hair. He groaned as he crushed her close, liking how her soft body yielded itself against his. His lips found her ear and he whispered hungrily, "I want more, too..."

She pulled back, just enough to look him in the eyes, and she nodded, those petal-pink lips parted ever so slightly. He cradled her in his arms, watching like a doomed man while she slowly traced one finger down her neck, then around one of her breasts...teasing him, encouraging him. With a guttural moan, he kissed her exposed shoulder, swearing he'd never tasted skin so sinfully soft before in his sorry life.

And he didn't stop there.

His lips pressed a path along her collarbone, then he kissed and licked the top mound of one of her breasts, the rest of which was still hidden behind this damn slip. *Have to see her.* With his teeth, he bit the lacy top of the slip and tugged it down, exposing a breast. He reared back, astounded at the sheer beauty of its creamy, pink-tipped loveliness. If he had any last thoughts of behaving like a gentleman, they self-destructed when she arched her back and pulled his head down to her swollen rosebud tip.

He circled it with his tongue, slowly, then closed in on the nipple, flicking its pebbled hardness with his tongue. When Robin released a tormented moan, desire shot through him like a blast of heat, igniting his carnal needs. He yanked up her slip and wedged his knee between her legs, ready to take her now. Here.

No.

With great effort, he reined himself back, releasing a long, agonizing groan. Gorged with need, he fought for self-restraint. He had to see her, feel her, taste her...but damn it all, he didn't want this to be over in one hot, out-of-control moment.

Robin's half-closed eyes flew open, giving him a questioning look. In ragged, halting breaths, she whispered, "I...want...I want..."

He wanted to explain he was forcing himself to take it slower, but before he could summon the words, she pulled out of his embrace.

Robin stared into his face. She felt hot and bothered and...confused! Did she have to *tell* him what she wanted? Hadn't the gimme-hot-stuff music, nothing-underneath-it slip, take-me-now gyrations spoken louder than words? Or was he afraid to take it further with Robin Lee, the girl from back home? Was she still, in part of Johnny's mind, the quiet, stuttering kid who depended on him to help her? Did it scare him to take it the next step, to become lovers?

Well, she'd let him know she was no longer that girl. She was a grown woman, with a woman's needs and desires. Looking him boldly in the eyes, she gripped the lacy edge of her slip bodice and pulled it down. Over her stomach, down her thighs, her legs, until she stepped out of it. She watched his eyes travel hungrily all over her and she smiled, enjoying her power as a woman. Holding the filmy slip in the air between them, she shook it a little, a little "come and get it" gesture, before she tossed it aside.

Then she stood before him, naked, her skin prickling with pleasure as Johnny's gaze consumed and devoured every inch of her.

"You're all pink and alabaster," he murmured, his hands clenching as though he was already kneading her flesh. "It's too bright," he said abruptly, crossing to the wall switch and flicking the switch. Only one light remained on, the lamp on her desk, which hazed the room in a low, shimmering glow.

Johnny returned and stood before her. Her heart pounded wildly. Perspiration dewed her body. She was on fire...ready to be Johnny's lover.

His fingers tunneled into her hair and he leaned over,

inhaling its scent. "Sweet, like you," he whispered huskily before his fingers trailed sensuously down the side of her cheek. Cupping her face, he looked into her eyes. "I don't have protection," he said quietly. He'd been so rushed earlier, he hadn't had time to get anything. Even if he had, he wondered if he would have prepared for sex. With other women, he always planned ahead. But with Robin, ah, with Robin, planning would have felt...manipulative, conniving...and he wanted to be a better man with her.

She blinked. "M-me neither."

Of course she didn't. He held her gaze for a long moment. "We'll be creative, then." He looked around the room, then turned back to her. Backing up, he crooked his finger, motioning her to follow.

5

CREATIVE? A delicious thrill washed over her. Creativity in lovemaking? She'd *never* been creative in that area, unless twisting oneself into a back-seat pretzel with her high school boyfriend counted. Despite the shadows in the room, she caught a naughty glint in Johnny's baby blues as he continued walking backward, urging her to follow him. This man undoubtedly knew love creativity from *A* to *Z*, and she was ready to start with the first letter and take her sweet, sweet time working her way through the alphabet.

Except…

She glanced toward the large windows that ran along the south wall of her apartment. Those windows were the reason why she'd rented this place—she loved the warmth of sunshine as it spilled in. Loved watching falling snow as it swirled and shifted into magical shapes. But mainly she loved looking up at the Colorado sky and knowing home and family weren't far away.

Looking outside was one thing but she didn't want someone looking *in* and see her being sexually creative!

When she'd rented the place, the landlord said the old brick building across the way was a former warehouse, now abandoned, but she'd often wondered if artists might have rented the space—she'd read somewhere how artists loved old abandoned warehouses, anyway. The space was cheap and big. Perfect for creating state-of-the-art paintings where the artists would smear themselves in colors then roll all over a huge canvas, their bodies' movements symbolizing the need for free expression in a rule-oriented world.

Not that she'd given it a great deal of thought, of course, but it seemed plausible.

At least where she stood, next to the hallway, she was well hidden from any voyeuristic, paint-smearing artists. But Johnny and his beckoning finger were now standing smack in front of the windows.

"Get that beautiful body over here," he instructed.

Oooo, his voice was so low, so hungry, he sounded as though he might devour every inch of her. Her heart raced, her body shook. All that stood in the way of being lovers with Johnny was her overactive imagination, with its make-believe midnight artists across the way. But she wasn't going to let that stop her from being the lover of Johnny Dayton, the man she'd spent half her lifetime fantasizing, dreaming about. She rolled back her shoulders. No way, no how.

But to be on the safe side, she'd ask him to close the blinds. She pointed toward the windows.

Johnny paused, then glanced out the windows. "Is there something outside?" He stepped right up to the window, obviously trying to see what she was pointing at. Moonlight sifted through the glass, coating him in a silvery sheen. Her breath caught in her throat. The moonlight played magic with Johnny. Doused his black hair with ethereal blue highlights, spun a silvery thread along the outline of his rugged silhouette.

"No one's out there," he said, turning toward her. He cocked his head, as though trying to analyze her concern. "Even if there was, that little piece of decoration you call a lamp barely sheds enough light for even Mick to see us...trust me, you're safe."

She stood, still awestruck by his presence, by the teasing tricks moonlight played. If she had a cogent thought, now that she knew they couldn't be seen, it was how to walk gracefully to him when her body was totally out of control—her lips trembled, her knees wobbled, and if that wasn't enough, her toes were tapping anxiously on the hardwood floor as though ready to peel out any moment. Thank God she was barefoot so he couldn't hear their gimme-love *tap, tap, tap.*

"You're safe," he repeated gently. "It's just you and me...and the moonlight."

You're safe. No man had ever cared to look beyond her silence and figure out what triggered her moods and concerns. Robin felt some part deep inside her soften and cave in, like an empty structure that no longer needed to protect what it held within. And in the next moment, she realized something else. She realized that she *trusted* Johnny. Trusted him with her emotions, her body...

...with her heart.

She started walking toward him.

"Slower," he whispered huskily, doffing his jacket and tossing it over the back the recliner.

There was a tingling in the pit of her stomach as she slowed her pace, watched him watching her. Miraculously, her toes behaved, leading the way slowly...

"You look like a Gibson Girl," he whispered, "beautiful, luscious...like a porcelain figure, washed in pearly moonlight..."

She smiled tentatively. Gibson Girl? She had no idea what that meant, but thrilled at his other words. *Beautiful. Luscious. Washed in pearly moonlight. Oooooo. He's a poet.* He knew she loved reading and writing, but did he also know her passion for poetry? A phrase from one of Emily Dickinson's poems ran through her head. "Twas my one Glory/Let it be remembered/I was owned of Thee..." And so would Robin soon be owned by Johnny, body and soul, as the man of her dreams made love to her, made her body his own.

She reached him and stopped. Mere inches separated their bodies. She could feel his heat, smell his scent. She darted a nervous tongue at her bottom lip, wanting more, but for the life of her, it was all she could do at this moment to stand still she was so hypnotized by his presence and by the anticipation of what was to come.

Johnny pulled off his shirt and tossed it onto the nearby recliner on top of the jacket. Robin stared at his masculine chest, her breasts heaving as she struggled to breathe. If the moonlight played sensual tricks with his form, the light from the nearby lamp was downright wicked. Its amber haze burnished his skin and wove threads of gold into his black chest hair. Laser-hot sensations fired through her as she imagined how it'd feel to smother her face in that hair, taste its silky texture, and although she was ready to jump in and go for every single sensation she'd just imagined, she didn't. Not yet. Johnny had said "slower" and that's what she wanted—to take it slow, to let every sensation burn into her memory...to always remember, always remember...

A long, thick silence drew out between them as she did a slow inventory of his torso. His shoulders were broad and nicely muscled. Of course, Johnny had always been an outdoors kind of guy. She remembered how he and Bud loved to race their bikes in the Rockies' foothills, coming home sweaty and tanned.

Her gaze dipped. His pleasure of the outdoors also showed in a taut midriff. Even in this dim light, she spied the ridges of muscle through dark hair that teased a path downward and ended at his belt buckle.

If his chest was this good, what lay below?

Feeling almost greedy with anticipation, she glanced back up and caught him doing a similar inventory of her. His eyes glittered as a sinful grin played with his lips. Yes, indeed, he was looking her over, mentally exploring her secret places.

And she loved it.

Being the object of a man's desire was a powerful aphrodisiac. The golden haze of the light seemed to intensify with her arousal. She straightened so he could see everything, inviting his fantasies, wanting him to explore her more...and he accepted the unspoken invitation. His gaze boldly raked over her, settling on her breasts, then dropping lower to the cleft where her thighs joined. And there his gaze lingered, causing desire to flood through her entire body.

She wanted more, *now.* She didn't care if they were in front of a window—they could be in a department store display window and she wouldn't care—she had to touch, feel, taste him now, now, *now.* With a moan, she speared her fingers into his thick chest hair, relishing the texture of the luxurious carpet. It felt surprisingly silky despite its mass. She rubbed and fondled the thick strands, following their path across his pecs, down his stomach...

Then, with her hands on his waist, she leaned closer so her breasts gently pressed against that luxurious mat of hair, and rubbed her nipples ever so gently against him. Heat and electricity shot through her, straight down to her groin.

"Oh, baby," Johnny groaned. Gripping her shoulders, he gently pushed her back and stared at her breasts. "Moonlight becomes both of you," he whispered, flashing a mischievous look at Robin before returning his gaze to her breasts. "God, you are so...they are so..."

He was tongue-tied? She'd adored how he'd made her feel so luscious, so gorgeous, but for him to have trouble *speaking* while looking at her body. Well, she didn't know whether to laugh or cry. But she did neither as a more sober thought hit her—she and Johnny shared a special world where words weren't necessary.

He reached out and placed one fingertip on a nipple, and any remaining thoughts blew away on a lusty release of breath. He gently pinched the distended nipple, then with his other hand lightly kneaded the other. Although she was able to remain standing, the lower half of her body writhed in pleasure as sensations rocketed through her. And when he pulled both breasts together, tight, and suckled on both nipples at the same time, she dropped back her head and panted, her toes curling in ecstasy.

Then his hands slid down her sides, slowly, and encircled her waist. As though waking from a euphoric reverie, she slowly lifted her head and looked up into that handsome, shadowed face. She shivered from the memory of his mouth, the heat of his fingers spread around her middle. He said they'd be creative? This man wasn't merely creative, he was a magician. God, what he could do with a pair of hands, a pair of lips and a set of needy breasts....

Just thinking what those lips could do elsewhere made her wobbly. If she was having trouble standing, well obviously she needed to lean against something, the sooner the better.

Linking her fingers through his, Robin wove a lazy path across the room to her desk, a chuckling Johnny in tow, murmuring something about "ladies first." The music continued in the background, sultry and hot. *Just like me*, Robin thought. Sultry and hot and on her way to more, more, more. As she passed the birdcage, Mick twittered a bit, then resumed eating his dinner. Reaching the desk, Robin shoved the ergonomic chair away with her foot, then leaned against the edge of the desk, positioning Johnny between her straightened legs. Now that they were right next to the lamp, she got the full glorious view of his torso.

"Oh-h-h my-y-y..." She wasn't stuttering, just breathing out the exclamation as any enthralled woman would facing such a gorgeous hunk of male body. Before, with a hint of light, his chest hair had looked dark, felt thick. But now that they were closer to the lamp, she saw how the chest hair ran wild across his bronzed pecs, then swept down his stomach in an inverted triangle, pointing toward his midriff...

Her inventory stopped on his belt buckle, a classy looking silver number on what looked to be a belt made of some kind of plush leather. She'd wondered before what lay behind that belt and by damn, she was going to find out. She wanted it *now*.

She grabbed the buckle as Johnny's strong hands clasped her wrists. His hold was firm, strong.

"They're not coming off."

She looked up at him and pleaded with her eyes.

"Don't give me that look." He tried to sound stern, but Robin also heard his amusement. He *liked* how much she wanted him.

"The pants stay on." He raised her hands and kissed them. "It's the best form of protection I can think of on the fly." He grinned. "No pun intended."

Robin giggled and curled her toes. Damn he looked sexy, stripped to the waist, gilded all over with tawny light, playing tough guy. She knew damn well he wanted her in every way, just as she wanted him, but at least one of them was being responsible.

"Don't move," Johnny whispered, then disappeared into the room's darkness.

Move? It'd taken all her wits to walk from the window to here. Wits that were on a serious shortage right now just imagining what creative thing was to come. She strained to hear over the music, a slow, heated song of lusty longing. Add Johnny's muffled noises from somewhere across the room, and Robin's imagination went into overdrive. What was he getting to add to his already exceptionally creative moves? Ropes? Handcuffs?

Okay, so her imagination was getting the better of her. If a man was too rushed to drop by the store and buy protection, he was definitely too rushed to drop by the local sex shop and pick up a pair of handcuffs.

Johnny appeared in the pool of lamplight, gripping two of the floor pillows.

Pillows?

He tossed the green one onto the floor next to the desk, but continued holding the pink one. She glanced from it to the sexy look on Johnny's face, and her body heat rose. She felt so hot, no doubt her skin color matched the fuchsia color of that pillow.

Johnny checked out the desk behind her. "You and coffee," he teased huskily, moving the cups to the side with his free hand, then setting the water and seeds on the floor. She thought about last night when she'd approached his table with the coffeepot, but ended up pouring herself on him, and she grinned.

"Did I mention I like your choice of books?" he murmured, gently placing them on the floor, as well. "Fantasy...wild and imaginative, just like you."

Me, wild?

Well, she had tackled him on a tabletop. And lunged at his belt buckle.

"Stand up," he ordered gently, and she did. Johnny placed the pink pillow on the desk. Then he squeezed her around the waist and lifted her, effortlessly, placing her rump onto the pillow.

She held her breath, not wanting to admit she was more than a bit embarrassed that he'd *lifted* her. Forget being buck naked, or the little sexy surprises he obviously had in store, this man *lifted* her as though she weighed nothing. *I'm wild and light!*

"Those thoughts in your head are going about a million miles an hour." Johnny stood before, his arms crossed over his chest as he scrutinized her face. He arched one eyebrow in a question. "Are we...doing what you want?"

Was he kidding? They were doing what she'd wanted for most of her life! She nodded so fast, his face split into a grin.

He leaned forward, pressing both of his palms flat on the desk on either side of her. His face was inches from her own and she nearly swooned at his masculine, musky scent. "Whatever you're thinking," he whispered, grazing her cheek with his own, the words hot against her ear. "It doesn't matter. All that matters is you and me...and what we're going to enjoy."

When his knowledgeable lips licked and blew warm puffs of air into the hollow behind her lobe, she groaned, clutching the edge of the desk. Each exhalation of warm breath prickled her skin and sent her senses swirling—her only momentary reprieve when he shifted his lips and trailed them, ever so slowly, across her cheek until they grazed her mouth.

"You want more?" His words were hot, husky against her lips.

"Uhhh-huhhh..." At some point, she'd lost control of this situation. Probably the moment he stepped inside her apartment.

He touched her lip with his tongue and ran it teasingly along the inside of her top lip. "More?" he teased.

She pressed her lips forward, ready for a full-on, I-want-more kiss, but he eased back his head, keeping his lips just out of reach. She shot him a question with her eyes and he responded with a cocky smile, his blue eyes burning like gas flames.

Was he playing hard to get at a moment like this?

Well, if what you want is what you get, she was gonna get more. She pressed her case, puckering her lips, and moved forward, determined and aching to get more.

She released a prolonged, achy moan as their mouths finally met, branding their need on each other. His hand glided up the back of her neck and he burrowed his fingers into the back of her hair, holding her in place. And if she thought they'd kissed before, she was a fool, because *now* he really kissed her.

A bolt of shock and pleasure shot through her as he plunged his tongue deep inside, deepening the kiss, filling her with his strength, his passion. She opened her mouth wider, wanting more, taking more as hot desire pooled in her loins. Fiery and sweet, they made love to each other's mouths for long minutes....

When he pulled away, he was breathing hard. His gaze left hers and traveled down her body, down to the triangle of golden curls between her legs before he raised his gaze back to hers.

"You have a beautiful body, Robin."

For a crazy moment, she thought she'd cry. Yes, he'd told her she was beautiful, but this time it was more than the words—it was how he said it. Reverentially, as though he'd never seen a woman's body before. He made her *feel* beautiful, totally completely beautiful, in a way she never had before.

Johnny had never seen a woman so taken aback by a simple compliment. The look on her face was so grateful, so trusting, he felt a warmth fill him that was different than the heat of passion. This woman touched him in a way no woman ever had before. With the simplest look, he felt his guard slipping, which terrified him even as it enthralled him.

Something touched his leg and he looked down. Robin's toes were pressed against his jean-clad thigh, playfully prodding him. He looked at her face and smiled at the twinkle in her eyes. And as they stared at each other, the teasing toes brushed lightly over his crotch, bringing him to a hard, fast arousal.

He grabbed her foot and held it midair. "I told you, the pants stay on," he whispered, liking—no, loving—her show of lusty need. "We'll save that for next time..." He massaged her foot, pressing his thumb slowly up the arch to the toes, which he raised to his lips. As he suckled her toes, she leaned back and groaned, offering him a mouthwatering view of her body and the pleasure she was enjoying. Damn, she looked delicious. Softly rounded, nicely proportioned, glazed with that honeyed light. And from this angle, with her foot suspended in the air, he had a thrilling view of the crevice between her legs, all full and pink like an unfolding flower.

He ran his free hand down her leg and skirted his fingers lightly over her opening, briefly touching her nub. He loved her sharp intake of breath and the way she arched her back. He looked up at her breasts, full and round, and let his fingers trail up her torso to those mounds where he ran light, lazy circles around the nipples.

Robin writhed with pleasure as desire coursed through her, heating her blood. Instinctively, she arched her back higher, thrusting her breasts out, wanting more...wanting it so badly, she thought she'd damn near explode. Panting, she straightened, took Johnny's head with both her hands, and pulled him close. She ached for his mouth to take her, suckle her, and when he did, she gasped with pleasure. Then, still holding his head, she guided it to the other breast, which he eagerly took in his mouth and sucked slowly, deliberately, groaning as she gasped louder.

Then he straightened and stepped back, giving her such a bad-boy look, she felt her insides plummet. She loved that expectant look in his eye, the way a lock of hair fell over his brow, the swelling of his chest as he sucked in deep breaths. She'd never felt the power in being a woman before, and it felt damn good.

She slid her hand down her breast, down her tummy, to her thigh where she let her fingers slowly stroke her skin before she moved her finger to the soft, wet center between her legs. He watched, his eyes glistening, as she gently slipped her finger into the wet folds. She'd never been this way with a man, and it felt deliciously wicked...and wonderfully safe. Open to him this way, she realized in the deepest sense how much she trusted Johnny.

He smiled. A slow, sexy smile that said he'd received her message loud and clear.

He reached over, grabbed the pillow on the floor, and tossed it to a spot in front of her on the floor. And here she thought she was showing him what she wanted but at that moment, she realized this is what he'd been planning all along.

He dropped to his knees and kissed the inside of each thigh, then gently moved her hand from where it massaged her nub, replacing her motions with his mouth.

Robin gasped and fell back onto the pillow. Waves of heat enveloped her as her entire body succumbed to his expert manipulations. She burrowed her fingers into his thick hair, pressing herself against him as his wicked tongue gave her pleasure as she'd never known before. Pleasure so exquisite, it bordered on torture. Sweet, hot torture. Currents of electricity shot across her skin as she thrashed and sobbed, aching for release. And then, for an exquisite moment, the world stilled as though she were on a precipice before her entire body exploded in a crescendo of pleasure.

Afterward, he leaned over her and enveloped her in an embrace as his lips gently kissed her cheeks, her neck, her lips. They stayed like this for a long moment, their bodies close, so close, she could feel their beating hearts.

And she wanted to tell Johnny everything she felt, how he'd fulfilled her every fantasy, how he'd made her a woman, but she also knew words weren't necessary. Instead, she held him tight so he could feel her pounding heart, which pulsed a message over and over. "Thank you, thank you..."

6

JOHNNY BLINKED his eyes, trying to ward off the assault of bright light. Had he fallen asleep with all the lights on, again? One of the bad habits he'd developed over the last few years, but with back-to-back meetings, the only time left to review business reports was right before bed. Unfortunately, he often didn't make it that far, and would wake up in his den, sprawled across the leather sofa amid papers and pens, the TV droning in the background.

That is if William, his butler, hadn't gotten up in the wee hours to check on Johnny and doused the lights and TV, as well as tossed a blanket across the sleeping Johnny. He had hired William to run his household, but more and more, William seemed to be running Johnny's life. Like a mother in a three-breasted suit. Ensuring Johnny ate right, took his vitamins, and calling taxis for the various dates who stumbled into the kitchen the morning after.

Fortunately, William wasn't perfect or Johnny would have long ago lost his mind. William loved soap operas and the dog races, the latter a bit too much. On more than one occasion, he'd asked Johnny to "spot" him a twenty, which was quietly repaid the next payday.

Johnny squinted into the stinging sunlight. Okay, maybe William had doused the lights, but he usually closed the drapes, too. Not like William to forget a detail like that. And since when did the TV make an incessant chirping sound?

Johnny dared to open both eyes and flinched at the sight of a large rectangular window ablaze with sunlight. *That's not my den window.*

Chi-i-r-rp!

Johnny winced and slid a glance toward the sound. Across the room, a green-headed bird stared and chirped again at Johnny. He looked down. He was lying on a zipped-open sleeping bag, covered with a blanket. His stomach clenched as he flashed back to years ago, when he and his brother slept just like this in a corner of the living room. Other memories surfaced. Johnny waking up in the middle of the night, discovering his brother gone, and throwing on some jeans and a shirt to go looking for him. Or waking to find his father stumbling in the door, cursing, oblivious to the world...and his two kids.

Johnny could have taken the easy way out and moved in with another family—hell, several times Bud's mom had invited Johnny to move in, take the bottom bunk bed in Bud's room—but Johnny loved his kid brother, Frankie. Maybe the world had given up on Frankie, but Johnny hadn't. He'd once mentored Frankie in algebra and had been blown away how quickly Frankie understood and manipulated numbers. And how many times had Johnny witnessed Frankie wooing an entire room like some kind of showman—the kid had the makings of a leader. No, Johnny couldn't have left home, no matter how bad it got, because he couldn't stand the thought of no one believing in Frankie.

But Johnny's failure to salvage his family, especially his kid brother, still ached like a raw wound.

Soft singing drew him back to the present. Scrubbing his hand across his face, Johnny listened to the feminine voice. *Robin.* Was that an old Stones tune she was singing? Sure enough, he caught a riff, words about "going home." He could never go home again, although she certainly gave the words an appealing, melancholy twist.

Sweet, melancholy Robin. What lay in *her* heart? Why was she in Denver? Did she want to return to Buena Vista—to go home?

He gazed at the framed pictures on the wall, picking out Robin in each one.

And as he looked at her face, last night's memories rushed back on waves of heat. Her body, all pink and alabaster, draped across the desk as though it were a pedestal. And he, paying homage like a love-starved suitor, bending to her needs. He rubbed his fingers along the satiny edge of the blanket, recalling the softness of her skin. His lower body ached with the memories...and with his own unsatisfied need.

But he hadn't wanted to do more last night. Not even when she teased him with strategic caresses after he'd lifted her off the desk. He'd whispered that next time, they'd indulge *both* their desires to a mutual gratification.

The scent of coffee filled the room and he looked up. There stood Robin, her unkempt blond hair framing her sleepy, happy face. She looked more beautiful with a freshly washed face than most women did with all that war paint. That was something else unique about Robin—she didn't need to wear a mask in the world.

He looked her up and down. She'd put on a long pink T-shirt, nearly the color of the pillow he'd propped her on last night, with scripted letters printed on it. *There is no frigate like a book/To take us Lands away...* Underneath there appeared to be a signature. He stared at it, trying to decipher the cursive script.

"Emily Dickinson," Robin said softly.

He looked up, delighted she'd spoken. "So Emily is one of your favorite poets." He'd purposefully phrased it rhetorically so Robin could choose whether or not to respond. Years ago, he'd seen the play *The Belle of Amherst*, a one-woman show depicting the life of Dickinson. The prolific poet led a deceptively quiet life, her passion pouring into her poems. Not unlike the woman who stood before him now.

Robin held up two mismatched steaming mugs.

"Decaf?" he asked. "After all, I don't want to get jittery."

She grinned, obviously recalling his words at the diner.

"Doesn't matter." He rolled onto one elbow and reached for a cup with his other hand. "Doctor says one cup of octane is okay, but after that, I have to go un-leaded." He accepted the offered cup from Robin, whose eyes held a question.

He set his cup on the floor and pulled back the blan-ket so she could sit next to him on the sleeping bag. He glanced behind them and noticed they'd shared the one oversize orange pillow during the night. He eased to a standing position and crossed the room to retrieve the green and pink pillows. When he saw the pink one still on the desk, with the green one on the floor, he felt him-self grow hard remembering what it had been like to be on his knees, giving her pleasure.

He grabbed both pillows and headed back to the sleeping bag, where he plumped all three pillows in one heap. When he dropped the pillows next to the sleeping bag, he caught Robin's gaze roaming over his body, the look on her face making his arousal tighten even more. Finally her visual inventory landed on his blue stretch underwear. Her breathing increased as she stared, without blinking, at the evident bulge. When she looked up, and found him observing her, pink flooded her cheeks.

"What is it about you and coffee?" He winked, enjoy-ing the color in her cheeks deepening to red. "When-ever you get near the stuff, things seem to get out of hand, fast." He chuckled, but didn't sit down, silently daring her to look again.

She did. A quick down and up, as though to make sure it was still there.

"I told you we'll wait." God, as though that were

easy. If he had protection, he'd take her now. Yank up that pink number and... He eased in a slow, steadying breath. "Next time, it'll be for both of us."

He sat down, plumped the pillows into a heap, and leaned back. Nice. They made a surprisingly comfortable backing. After they drank in silence for a few moments, Robin gently touched his arm.

He looked into her shiny eyes, now a bright green like the lush spring fields back home. "Why one cup?" she finally asked, her words spoken with great care.

She hadn't stuttered again. Maybe it was his male pride, but he took full credit for that. *She's feeling more comfortable with me.* "One cup?" He'd been so caught up in congratulating himself, he'd lost the thread of the conversation. "Oh—why did the doctor say only one cup. Well, it's for my health..."

The green in her eyes darkened.

"Stress and coffee don't mix. I have too much of the first, so I need less of the second."

She frowned, obviously wanting more explanation. "And?"

He blew out a gust of air. He never discussed his health issues—or any personal issues for that matter—with anyone. One, it scared investors and board members if they thought their CEO might have stress-related health issues, which he didn't have, well not really. A heart murmur was manageable—lots of people had them.

Two, it sure as hell would scare employees if they thought their leader had failing health. Employees looked to their leader the way sailors looked to the captain of a ship—they needed to know someone strong was at the helm, guiding them.

Robin blinked, took a sip of her coffee, her big eyes staring at him over the rim of her cup. Finally, after lowering the cup, she said softly, "What do you do?"

He never thought just to hear someone speak comfortably, fluently, would give him such joy. It was as though an invisible hand had reached inside and squeezed his murmuring heart. Robin touched him like that. Deeply, profoundly because she cared for him as *Johnny*, not the CEO. Again, he realized he didn't want her to know what he did for a living because the job had toughened him, changed him. He wanted her to see him as the outgoing, devil-may-care Johnny he once was.

And with a need that bordered on painful, he yearned to be that man again.

"I'm a...lineman," he said quickly before taking a slug of coffee. It wasn't a lie. Not really. After all, as CEO, he had to spin lines. Every day he choose words that kept the investors happy, omitted words to keep the board satisfied, emphasized words to keep the employees motivated.

"Lineman?" Cupping her hands around her coffee mug, she continued staring at him with those big eyes.

Well, when she opened up, she sure asked a lot of questions. Now she wanted to know what he *did* as a lineman. Well, he knew what OpticPower's linemen did. "I fix cable and install optic fiber," he said quickly.

Okay, he wasn't exactly pretending anymore. He was lying. It disgusted him to hear himself lie to Robin.

"Wh-which company?"

She'd stuttered. Had she sensed his lie? "Local," he said offhandedly, which wasn't an answer but he wanted to slide off this subject. Fast. "And you?" He looked up at the pictures, then back to Robin. "What are you doing in the big city of Denver? Surely you didn't move here to work in a diner."

Hurt clouded her eyes and he regretted stumbling so inelegantly into that question. "I'm sorry—"

But she held up her hand, cutting off the apology. She breathed in and out, then murmured, "DU."

Denver University. Interesting. "What are you studying?"

She smiled sadly and held up one hand, her thumb and forefinger forming an *O*.

Zero? She was studying *nothing*? Realization flashed through him. For some reason, she was no longer a student. He had a hundred questions. *What happened? Are you returning? If not, why stay working at a diner? Why not go home?* At moments like this, it was damn frustrating to not converse freely with her. Yes, he could read things in her eyes, but right now, her look of disappointment wasn't enough to help him understand exactly why she was in the predicament she was in. Plus he'd wondered about her car—wanted to offer to help her, but knew she'd never accept a handout. *Too much pride.* But he couldn't judge her—when it came to keeping secrets, she reminded him of himself. With time she'd open up...hopefully. Meanwhile, he'd ask Shelia to do some discreet investigation, track down Robin's car, and quietly pay the bill. He'd tell the auto repair place or Shelia how to explain the returned car—after all, Johnny was a lineman.

In the silence, he heard Mick occasionally ruffle his feathers or emit a quick chirp...and there was another sound. A steady *tick, tick, tick*. He looked over and saw a plastic cat clock above the bookcase, its tail swishing, ticking, for every second. Its whiskers were the hands of the clock. Seven-twenty.

"I'm late," Johnny stated. He had to hustle if he wanted to catch the light-rail and make it to the board meeting on time. Good thing Shelia always kept several clean, pressed suits available in his office. He slugged back the rest of the coffee and stood. Grabbing his clothes, he began putting them on.

"I'll call you soon," he said, tossing on his T-shirt. It was the truth, but he caught the telltale worry in Robin's eyes. She wasn't sure if he was telling the truth. Could he blame her? She sensed he hadn't told the truth with that damn "lineman" line, but that was his *only* lie to her.

He clamped tight his jaw, wishing like hell he hadn't said it, though. Maybe he'd learned to spin the right lines to protect his company, but in his gut, he knew he wasn't protecting his relationship with Robin with them.

He wasn't even protecting himself because his lies would never make him into Johnny again.

WHAT WAS Johnny hiding?

After he left, Robin sat curled up in her recliner, looking at the vast Colorado sky through her window. Clouds had moved in over the last few minutes, their mass of white making it nearly impossible to see the blue sky. It was like trying to see the real Johnny.

And yet, she *knew* the real Johnny. Their lovemaking last night had been real. As well as the way he'd cuddled her all night long. She'd never known how delicious it could be to fall asleep intermeshed with a man's warmth and scent. And yet, despite their growing closeness, she had a gnawing uneasiness inside her. Because just as she saw patches of blue in the sky above, she saw pieces of the Johnny Dayton from back home, but she really didn't know Johnny *now*.

She wanted to know what lay behind that wary look she sometimes saw in his eyes, know why he seemed so guarded, secretive. Where had the charismatic, extroverted Johnny gone? Asking him simple questions— like where he worked—pushed some kind of hot button. That look on his face had grown more guarded when he'd said "lineman."

Plus, what kind of man who laid cable for a living wore a fancy gold watch? The only explanation to that little mystery was if Johnny had purchased that expensive item during a "macho moment." Her brother had had *plenty* of such "macho moments," including the summer he'd blown eight hundred dollars—his entire earnings from a summer flipping burgers—on a weekend in Vegas. Although that money was supposed to go toward Bud's college education, Robin's mother hadn't chewed him out. She'd simply said, "Life is about choices and the universe gave you this experience so next time you'll make the right choice." And Bud had. The next summer, he applied his summer earnings toward earning a certificate in accounting.

Maybe it was the same for Johnny. Maybe he blew an entire paycheck on some slick, macho watch. Guys did things like that. It was what they did with their second chances that counted.

Although a "macho moment" didn't explain why he was so guarded. Too bad Johnny and Bud had lost touch—if they'd stayed in contact, she could just pick up the phone and call her brother, see if he couldn't enlighten her about Johnny's history since he left Buena Vista.

But no one back home had stayed in contact with Johnny after he left for college, although everyone knew what happened to his family. How his kid brother, Frankie, ended up in county jail before disappearing to Utah. How Mr. Dayton, Johnny's dad, spent every night drinking at Billy's Bar before stumbling home, barking insults at anyone who crossed his path.

And how Mr. Dayton was discovered one morning next to the road, dead. Heart attack, the doctor had said, but everyone in town blamed the booze.

Johnny's dad had died the same year as her mom's car accident. Robin had been too busy taking care of her mother to attend Mr. Dayton's funeral, although she'd wondered if Johnny had returned to Buena Vista to lay his father to rest. According to townsfolk, however, Johnny never made an appearance. Robin knew Johnny's home life had been difficult, but it seemed incomprehensible that he wouldn't at least go to his father's funeral. At the time, Robin's mom had said, "Some people can't forgive themselves." Robin hadn't wanted to pursue the conversation because the words took on special significance for Robin. She couldn't forgive herself for her mom losing the court case.

Robin gave her head a shake, not wanting to dwell on the past. This morning, she wanted to think about Johnny and why he'd changed. Maybe he told the truth about being a lineman, she mused. *And he acted oddly because he feels ashamed of what he does for a living.* After all, he'd managed to earn a scholarship, like she had, for college. Some school on the Pacific coast. Funny, she hadn't heard much about him after he left Buena Vista. Obviously, if he ended up a lineman, his career goals had crashed and burned. Sort of like Robin dropping out of college.

Robin wasn't a New Age kind of person, and had sometimes scoffed at her mom's comments about how "the universe" gave signs about this or that. But when Robin thought about how her and Johnny's paths had crossed—at a time when they were both struggling— she couldn't help but wonder if maybe the universe did indeed have a special purpose for their meeting again. Maybe they were thrown together because, in some way, they each felt like a failure.

Br-ring. Br-ring.

Robin stared at the caller ID, next to the phone on the side table. She never answered the phone unless she saw her mom's or brother's name. This time the caller ID displayed the name "Suzanne Doyle." Professor Doyle? Robin's favorite professor at the university!

Robin picked up the phone. "H-hello?"

"Robin?"

Professor Doyle's voice. Robin had missed that soft Southern accent. "Yes?"

"This is Suzanne Doyle... You took my class in communications at DU and I want you to know, first, how very sorry I am you dropped out of school." When there was no response, Professor Doyle added, "I never told students their rating in the class, but because of the circumstances, I want you to know you were my number one student."

All the angst and hurt at her sudden departure had weighed heavily on Robin's heart. She'd never had the chance to tell anyone how some of the college requirements, such as speaking in class or giving oral reports, were devastating for her. She never had the chance to tell Professor Doyle how much Robin had *loved* her class, *loved* how the professor inspired students about writing and communications. But the words lodged in Robin's throat, like a rock.

"Robin...you still there?"

Robin swallowed, hard. "Yes, Prof-f-f—"

"Call me Suzanne," she interrupted gently. There was a beat of silence before she continued. "The second thing I wanted to say is—I have a proposal for you."

Robin gripped the phone and listened intently.

"You were always a wonderful writer. How would you like to earn some money writing a speech?"

Robin writing a speech? Earning money? Without thinking, she emitted a gleeful whoop.

Suzanne chuckled. "Good. That's what I was hoping. Do you have a computer and modem?"

"No."

"Not an issue. Let's make arrangements for me to drop off a loaner laptop, show you how to use it and explain a bit about the assignment..."

The rest of the words blurred into a happy flow as Robin jotted down Professor Doyle's—*Suzanne's*—phone number, what time she'd drop off a loaner laptop from the university. Fortunately, Suzanne had Robin's home address on file, and could look up directions on the Internet, so Robin didn't have to explain how to get to her apartment.

After Robin hung up, she wrapped her arms around herself, too happy for words. Writing—for money! She reflected how just a few days ago her life had been in the pits. She thought she'd blown it, sort of like her brother's "macho moment" although she supposed hers had been a "matriculation moment." Giggling at her play on words, she skipped into the kitchen and helped herself to a few foil-wrapped candies she always kept in the bottom wire basket.

And as she savored the delicious taste, she also savored how, just like her brother, Robin had been given a second chance, too.

"YOUR GRAY SUIT is pressed and hanging in your office," announced Shelia as Johnny trotted toward his office door.

"Sorry," he said, pausing next to his executive assistant's desk. "I know I'm late."

"*Late?*" She made a huffing sound as though that word didn't *even* describe the seriousness of the situation. Shelia flicked her wrist and stared at the Chaumet, mother-of-pearl-face watch he'd bought for her last Christmas. He knew she never splurged on such luxuries for herself—and he knew, despite her demure "thank you" upon receiving the gift, that she downright coveted it. In fact, over the past nine months, she'd developed the annoying habit of checking the time at every single opportunity, which, he'd guessed, she'd been doing every other minute for the past hour.

"It's eight-fifty-two," she said matter-of-factly, staring at the watch. She looked up, her gray eyes flashing impatience, although he knew she was curious as hell what'd made him late. "The entire board of directors is waiting for you and you look as though you just—"

"—tumbled out of bed?" he offered.

She paused, obviously caught off guard but determined not to show it. He loved their interplay—he could be the bad-boy CEO, and she could be the amused-but-stern mother. For a guy who grew up with essentially no adult supervision, he'd ended up with two mothers—William and Shelia. Suddenly, a thought hit him.

"Do you like dog racing, Shelia?"

She looked at Johnny as though he lost his mind. Ignoring his non sequitor, she motioned toward his sleek black leather briefcase perched on the edge of her desk. "Everything's in your briefcase. Production stats, service metrics and a memo from Christine on the new testing structure."

He did a double take. "Did she try to fire Brad?"

Shelia gave him a knowing look. "Not yet..."

Shelia knew exactly what Johnny was really asking, because Shelia knew everything that went on in the business. She was like Grand Central Station, sitting outside the CEO's office, reading all his e-mails, answering his phones, watching his senior managers play jungle warfare. Undoubtedly, Christine had manipulated that memo so it sounded as though she wanted to build a stronger test organization, but embedded within her words would be pointed references to a "change in management," which meant firing Brad. And Christine had probably e-mailed the memo to the board prior to today's meeting.

"Damn her anyway," Johnny said, thinking of Christine's well-plotted power play.

Shelia made a disgruntled sound. "She's determined to fire Brad."

"Yeah, and that bullshit memo doesn't help." Words, words, words. He never trusted them, hell, most of the time he didn't even trust his own.

"And one more thing," Shelia said. "Penny called again."

He puffed out an exasperated breath. In business, one

never issued an ultimatum unless prepared to live with the consequences. Someone should have told Penny that little rule before she'd issued Johnny her ultimatum of marriage or nothing. Because he'd picked nothing. He raked his hand through his hair. But despite what happened, he didn't like knowing he'd hurt her.

"Send her a dozen roses with an apology note—"

"The usual sentiment?"

"The usual." Shelia had done this before—sent a lady roses, with a genteel note about his wishes for them to one day be friends. It was cliché, but some of his former relationships had actually turned into decent friendships, so it was worth the effort.

He opened the door to his office, but stopped before stepping inside, before stepping into the role of Jonathan P. Dayton, CEO. Suddenly, he felt exhausted with the pressure to always be the captain of the ship. In the past few days, he'd tasted his old life—the easygoing Johnny he used to be—and he wanted to feel like that again.

"Send some bagels and coffee to the board," he instructed Shelia. "Tell them to enjoy breakfast because I'll be a few minutes late..."

"How many is 'a few'?"

He mulled it over. "Ten."

"Ten?" Her voice rose a notch.

"No, fifteen."

"Fifteen?" He didn't think her voice could go *that* high.

"Yes," he affirmed, hearing a trace of what're-they-gonna-do-about-it in his voice—the same irreverent tone the old Johnny Dayton had. "I'm going to be *fifteen* minutes late. And if they complain, tell 'em a few minutes isn't the end of the world." He smiled to himself, liking his new—well, old but newly returned—attitude. Hell, maybe he'd make those board meetings start at 10:00 a.m. from now on. And instead of an hour, cut them back to thirty minutes. All that yakety-yak was mostly posturing and politicking, anyway. Thirty minutes would cut out the fat and get to the meat.

Shelia cleared her throat. "Well, since you're already late, I have another question. Shall I order another set of roses for...?"

He knew what Shelia meant. For the lady who caused him to rush in late with that just-tumbled-out-of-bed hair. Good ol' Shelia. Always thinking ahead. But for the first time in five years, Johnny heard something different in Shelia's voice. Something...wistful...

Johnny scanned her desk. It had always reminded him of the ice rink before an Avalanche game. And not just because it was glass on white plastic. Because it was pristine, untouched by anything personal. Like a picture of a family or a man. The more he thought of it, the more he knew she needed a day away from the office at the dog races, all expenses paid.

Shelia cleared her throat. "Did you want me to send—?"

"Oh, right," he said, recalling her question. "Wonderful suggestion, but don't send roses for this lady." Images of last night's lovemaking with Robin heated his memories. "Tell the florist to arrange a huge bouquet of lavender..." He thought of those big, vibrant throw pillows. "...and to throw in some wild orange and pink flowers as well. I'll jot down the lady's address on my way out..."

"And on the card," Shelia asked, "the usual sentiment?"

"No." He grinned. "Put 'To our next cup of hot coffee.'"

Shelia slid him a surprised look. "I'll have the flowers sent this afternoon. And don't forget you're traveling to Rhode Island this evening—a driver is picking you up at the office at eight—"

"Eight?" Damn, he'd forgotten about the trip to visit OpticPower's manufacturing plant in Rhode Island. "What time's the flight?"

"Nine."

He told Robin he would call her soon, which implied a date, but he'd forgotten about this damn business trip. He'd cancel it, but his Rhode Island staff had spent weeks scheduling the presentations, luncheons, dinners. "Delay my flight by a few hours—I need to take care of something before I leave."

"Mr. Dayton," said Shelia, "there is no later flight. The last one leaves Denver at nine o'clock, with a layover in New Orleans, where Joseph Finley, president of Media Cable, is adamant about meeting you—despite the late hour—to discuss a potential business deal. After that, you hop a red-eye to Rhode Island that gets you

in by 6:00 a.m., where an OpticPower vice president
will meet you..."

Sheila normally called him "Jonathan." When she
said "Mr. Dayton" she was getting wound tighter than
the inner workings of that watch he'd bought her. She'd
hinted before that if he had a corporate jet at his dis-
posal, these complicated travel arrangements could be
avoided. But Johnny preferred spending the corporation's money on things like an education program for
the employees rather than on an expensive jet.

"What time does the driver get here again?" he
asked.

"Eight. Your staff meeting is from six to—"

"I know." His weekly staff meetings were from six to
eight, but tonight he'd change that, too. "Tell everyone
the meeting will end at 7:30, at which time have my
driver here." He'd tell the driver to head straight to
Davey's Diner, because he had to see Robin, even if it
was only for a moment. Thinking of her lavender scent,
that pink-and-alabaster skin, those big expressive eyes,
he felt happier. Hell, damn right giddy.

"And one more thing," he said cheerfully to Shelia.
"Order a third bouquet—anything you think would
look beautiful—birds-of-paradise, exotic orchids, you
name it."

Shelia glanced at him over her shoulder, her gray
eyebrows arched in a question. "And to *whom* should
those be sent?"

"Why, to *you*, Shelia." As her eyes widened, he
winked at her. "And I also want you to take a day off

soon—not a vacation day, a sneak-out-of-the-office day. What we used to call 'playing hooky' back in school.''

''Playing hooky?'' she said, as though speaking a foreign language.

''Yes, I need you to go to the dog races with, uh, one of my colleagues.'' Well, William was a colleague, in a sense.

Whistling, Johnny strolled into his office and shut the door, but not before catching the look of stunned befuddlement on Shelia's face.

7

ROBIN SIGHED again as she stared at the most gorgeous bouquet of flowers she'd ever seen in her entire life. And this time, she wasn't being overly dramatic. It was the biggest, most lavish arrangement she'd *ever* seen— and it had been delivered to *her!* From the best guy in the world. Johnny.

She'd spent most of the last few hours this way, sprawled in her recliner, staring at the bouquet that she'd positioned on her desk so Mick could enjoy it, too. The little bird probably thinks he's been transported to a lush jungle, mused Robin.

Jungle. Isn't that how Johnny saw her? Wild, forbidden, lusty? Oh, yeah, he's got it right, she mused, kicking her fuzzy pink-slippered foot in time to the music, one of the Stones' rockin' tunes. Its deep, thrumming bass matched her pounding heart as she reread the note.

"To our next cup of hot coffee."

Whoa, baby! Soon they'd be more creative than just plain ol' hot coffee. Soon it'd be hot coffee with frothy milk, a dash of vanilla, maybe a tantalizing trace of mocha....

Now she had to lie back in the recliner and rest

awhile after thinking of all the creative combinations of hot coffee and hot love a bad boy and a jungle girl could concoct. Just the thought of what they'd do next time, or maybe tonight, made her pant.

Unfortunately, Johnny had left so quickly for work this morning, she hadn't had the chance to tell him that tonight was her night off. There was a chance he'd show up at Davey's Diner around midnight to walk her home, so she should somehow let him know she wouldn't be there. She'd checked her phone book and there was no listing for a Johnny Dayton or a J. Dayton, which meant she'd have to call Information to get his number. Oh, ugh. Who was she kidding? She *hated* using the phone—hated being on the spot to speak fluently to the automated response system. And she didn't want to call Davey's because she didn't know who she'd get on the line—and she didn't want to suffer through a stuttering, stammering conversation that'd go nowhere. *I'll just wait until he shows up here...which will be sometime after midnight.*

She checked the kitty clock on the wall. Seven-forty. What in the hell was she going to do with herself for four-plus more hours?

She snapped her fingers and grinned. *I'll plan on something sensually creative to wear!*

Her smiled dropped as her foot paused midkick. Something sensually creative? She didn't exactly have a Mata Hari wardrobe stashed away for special, sexy nights. But she must have *something* sexy lying around. She pursed her lips and contemplated possibilities.

Well, there was her old drill-team outfit that hung in the back of her closet. She could wear that short-short skirt with nothing on underneath—her foot started kicking again—but forget the sweater with the high school initials "BV" sewn on the front. She could envision herself opening the door, and his saying, "Give me a *B?*"

Not the effect she wanted. The *B* she did want followed *A* in the *A* to *Z* of Johnny's creative repertoire.

A memory from years ago flitted through her mind. A twelve-year-old Robin standing in the shadows outside a burger stand, watching Johnny in a convertible with several adoring, teenaged girls. Robin had envied how they teased and talked to Johnny. How she'd wished she could say such hot, flirty things, too.

Well, in the last few nights she'd learned that even if she didn't use her mouth to speak, her body certainly spoke up! Her moves told Johnny every tingling, sizzling reaction his touch had. But when it came time to make love to *him*, how would she know what he liked? Without asking him, how would she know where to touch him...*how* to touch him? With her high school boyfriend, they hadn't exactly put a lot of effort into foreplay—those back-seat romps had been like sex with the timer on.

And after the car accident, her boyfriend had drifted away, irritated that Robin was too busy for him anymore. But Robin didn't view taking care of her mom as "too busy"—it was her way of making amends to her mother. If only Robin had been able to speak on the stand instead of stammering incoherently about the accident, her mother would have had sufficient money for home care, additional physical therapy and other things that would have made their lives financially easier.

Knock, knock, knock.

Robin blinked, yanked back to the present. She shot a look at the kitty clock over the bookcase. Almost eight o'clock. Who would be knocking at this hour?

She got up, tiptoed to the front door, and peered through the peephole. Familiar sparkling blue eyes looked back at her.

Johnny!

Why was he here, now? Robin looked down at her old pink T-shirt with eyelet lace trim along the neckline, matching bikini pink underwear, her feet encased in fuzzy pink slippers with an ever-so-lovely dirt fringe. *The man of my dreams is on the other side of the door, and I look like a pink-dipped Q-tip.* Maybe it wasn't too late to find that drill-team outfit—

Knock, knock, knock. "Robin?" Johnny asked in that husky, sexy voice. "You there?"

She gulped. Darn it all anyway. By the time she found that old drill-team ensemble, whipped off her pink undies and zipped up the skirt, Johnny'd be gone!

"I—I—I'm h-h-ere," she yelped. *Sexy. Gotta look sexy. He sent me that jungle bouquet because I'm his jungle woman.* But what to do? She looked down. *I'll go for cleavage.* She grabbed the top of her T and, with all her strength, yanked. The old T-shirt ripped apart with an elongated *riiiippping* as she grunted in tandem.

"Robin?" Johnny asked. "You okay?"

She stared, wide-eyed, at the mess she'd made of her T-shirt. The thing had darn near ripped in half—either she was stronger than she thought or this shirt was older than she remembered. She stared, openmouthed, at her chest. She'd gone from slob to slut in five seconds flat.

"Robin?"

She couldn't open the door—not looking like a ripped-apart Q-tip. Fast, she had to do something to draw his attention to something sexier than a shredded outfit. Remembering how sexy Elizabeth Hurley looked in some movie with a wild mane of messy hair, Robin vigorously ruffled her own limp mane, praying it'd give her that Hurley Hussy look.

Knock, knock. "Robin?"

Okay, show time! Robin shoved open the two dead-bolts, flicked the knob lock, then, with a dramatic flourish, flung open the door.

Johnny stood there, looking like some kind of hot stud cover model who'd stepped right off the cover of one of those slick men's magazines like *GQ*. Maybe she only shopped at discount stores, but she loved to drool over those *GQ* cover boys...and here was one in the flesh, on her doorstep!

His dark hair and blue eyes complemented the double-breasted navy-blue suit with lapels that pointed toward his broad shoulders. Underneath that killer jacket, he wore a crisp blue-and-white striped shirt and a creamy tie decorated with bold red slashes. She licked her suddenly dry lips. *Only a passionate man would dare wear bold red slashes.* Her gaze continued down, past the creamy pocket square that peeked oh-so-casually out of his breast pocket, down the pleated pants—good Lord, did he iron the pleats to look like that?—to a pair of plush-looking loafers. Shoes that plush, with their soft buttery sheen, had to be leather...but *leather loafers?* Wasn't that a bit of overkill—like wearing silk overalls?

"Robin?"

She jerked up her gaze, wondering how long she'd been staring at his shoes and suddenly remembered she was wearing—horrors!—fuzzy pink slippers. With rings of dirt and patches of missing fuzz from years of wear and tear. Damn, damn, damn. She'd stamp her feet in frustration but it would only draw attention to them.

If only she could teleport back in time an hour and doll up in that cheerleader ensemble...

"You okay?" Johnny asked, concern creasing his face.

She nodded, knowing her eyes were filled with a look of utter mortification. Maybe it wasn't too late to do some damage control. With a shaky smile, she patted the mass of tousled hairs on her head, hoping that maybe, just maybe, he'd notice the Elizabeth Hurley hairdo over the rest of her ripped pink ensemble.

"Hey," he said softly, stepping inside. "Whatever you're worrying about, don't." He closed the door behind him, which shut with a soft click. "I don't have much time...only a few minutes."

A few minutes? She stiffened, trying not to act disappointed. Okay, utterly devastated. Maybe he'd taken one look at her and decided this fledgling relationship was a no-go and he'd better split, fast.

"Come here," he whispered, pulling her to him. He smelled good, all masculine and musky. Her cheek fell against his jacket and she rubbed her face against its texture, amazed how soft a man's suit could feel against bare skin. And as she nestled against him, she felt his lips trace a deliciously sensuous path up her cheek, all the way to her lobe, where he released a hot, teasing breath that made every single hair on her body rise to attention.

Suddenly, she didn't care what she was wearing, how her hair looked. All that mattered was his scent, his heated breath, the way his hands pressed firmly against her back, holding her tightly against him.

"Mmm, you feel good," he whispered. "Let me look at you."

Oh, God.

He stepped back, his hands still encircling her, as his glistening eyes grazed her from head to foot. "Nice," he said, stretching out the single word into a rugged sound of total appreciation.

Her mouth dropped open as she stared, in amazement, at this man who found her beautiful no matter what. *Pinch me, I'm dreaming.*

"It's eight," he finally said. "I stopped by the diner, thinking you'd be there. I have to be at the airport by nine…"

Airport? Nine?

"Business," he quickly explained, searching her eyes as though reading her distress. "I'll be back in a few days. I promise to call."

Her insides were like a roller coaster—one moment she felt up as his eyes glistened with desire and appreciation. The next, down, as she wondered if the "promise to call" was just a kiss-off line.

He gave her a questioning look. "You're worrying again."

You got it, buddy. Is this hello or goodbye?

His fingers ran up and down her back, pressing in spots she hadn't even realized ached from the tension she was holding. "Don't worry," he said gently, "I'm *really* going away on business and I'm *really* going to call. But I'm worrying about something, too."

My hair?

"You probably don't answer the phone, do you?"

The hair looks okay. Relieved, she nodded.

"Well," he said, obviously working through some plan in his head, "I don't know if the hotel name will appear in the caller ID, so I'll let the phone ring twice, then I'll hang up, wait a few seconds, then call again. You'll know it's me and you can answer."

A secret signal for just the two of them. *The way we communicate in other, special ways.* She'd never had this type of communication with a guy, where she was accepted as she was. Where the guy wanted to make it work, and created the means to do so. But maybe best of all, Johnny wouldn't make up *signals* unless he really meant he was going to call...really meant he wanted more of a...relationship. She grinned up at him, feeling ridiculously happy.

He arched an eyebrow, then lifted one side of his mouth in that devastatingly sexy grin that made her insides turn to liquid. "And after you pick up the phone, if you don't want to talk, that's okay. I'll say 'hi,' let you know how I'm doing, ask how you are... If you don't say anything, I'll know you're more comfortable not talking. Deal?"

She sucked in a deep breath. "Deal," she whispered.

"That's my girl." His gaze dropped again, stopping on the rip in her shirt. "Yes," he breathed, *"that's* my girl...my very sexy girl..." While he braced her back with one hand, he fingered the edges of her ripped T-shirt with the other, letting his fingers slide down the shredded opening, all the way to her exposed belly button which he teasingly circled with his finger. Then he trailed his index finger back up her tummy, playing his fingers across her torso, his light touches triggering currents of electricity that skittered crazily across her skin.

"I want you so bad," he murmured huskily, "I ache." In a swift movement, he grabbed the bottom of the T-shirt, bunched it in his fist, and for a heated moment, she thought he was going to rip the entire shirt off her body....

Instead, he tugged her closer so his lips grazed hers as he spoke. "When I get back," he whispered, "we're going to do it right. We're going to take our time, explore each other's bodies, please each other—" He slipped one hand into the ripped-apart shirt and gently pinched an erect nipple. Heat shot through her and she felt herself go wet. "—please each other in every possible way, all night long..."

That did it. Ms. Jungle Love turned to putty. She leaned back her head, barely able to breathe, groaning as his fingers teasingly tugged on first one hardened nipple, then the other. Then he pulled her face to his and he kissed her. A long, lingering kiss filled with hot promises.

At that moment, tasting her, holding her so close her soft, round body molded tantalizingly against his, he almost decided to cancel the trip. Almost. But knowing how many people depended on him stopped him from making the rash decision to stay. And oh, God, how he wanted to stay. As his tongue played with her mouth, exploring its sweetness, he wanted to just yank down those little pink panties, press her against the wall, and explode his need within her.

His kiss roughened as his body moved hard against hers, pushing, needing....

With a low groan, he pushed her away an arm's length and stared at the rosy flush that covered her chest, her cheeks. Felt the slick sweat forming on his own skin. If she whispered she wanted more at this moment, nothing could stop him from taking her right here...and he wished for it, craved it, wanted those luscious lips to form the words, express the want...

...and thank God she didn't say a word because, damn it, he wanted it to be *right* between them. Plus he'd promised the next time they made love, it would be for *both* of them. Because stronger than his physical need, he wanted to be her Johnny, the man she believed him to be, the man he *almost* believed he could be when he looked into her clear, trusting eyes.

Again, he couldn't find the words to express any of the emotions raging within him. And he thought he was the spin master? Robin had the power to make him hopelessly tongue-tied.

He cupped her face, warm from her desire, and stroked his thumb ever so gently across her cheek. He had to go, now, before he lost control. Shuddering loose a ragged breath, he opened the door and left.

Robin stood, teetering slightly, wondering why Johnny had vanished so quickly. She blinked as the door clicked shut, wondering if the last few minutes had been a figment of her imagination or the real thing. For a moment, she'd felt such an intense connection with Johnny—and then it dissolved the way a dream sinks back to the subconscious upon awakening.

Words from a Dickinson poem flitted through her mind. *Love's stricken "why" is all that love can speak.* Good ol' Emily sure had a way with words. Small poems that cut to the heart of a feeling or issue. Maybe, for the moment, Robin would have to settle for "why" and believe that one day she'd understand what was going on between her and Johnny.

She crossed to the window next to the front door and lifted one blind, ever so slightly, so she could see him one more time.

She saw him all right—sprinting down the stairs, like

some kind of dashing prince in that elegant suit. She'd been so caught up in that electrifying image of him when she'd opened the door, she hadn't thought about how odd it was that he wore expensive clothes. Clothes that had to be several "macho moments" rolled into one.

She searched the street, wondering which car he'd go to. Maybe he'd blown big bucks on a ridiculously expensive suit, but no way he'd gone "macho moment" when it came to his car. Most guys had one nice suit, but a car? Well, that more truly reflected a man's lifestyle. She scanned the cars, wondering if it was the red muscle car or maybe that beige economy number. She voted for the muscle car.

And soon she'd know because Johnny had reached the curb, but he stopped walking. What'd he do? Forget where he parked? Then a long, sleek black car pulled into view, eased to a stop in front of Johnny, and he jumped into the back seat.

Robin drew a shaky breath, hardly believing what she'd just seen. That was no mere *car*, that was a *limousine*. She opened the blinds, full, as though she hadn't seen clearly. Pressing her fingers against the cool, slick glass, she watched the limo ease down the street and disappear into the night.

Expensive clothes. Fancy watch. Limousine. The one thing she valued above all else in the world was truth... and she wasn't getting it from Johnny. A guy who earned his living laying cable couldn't possibly afford all the things Johnny surrounded himself with...she doubted even a *lifetime* of "macho moments" could afford the things he seemed so at ease with, as though he was accustomed to them, on a daily basis.

Robin's insides plummeted again into that crazy roller-coaster ride—up and down—as she wondered what was real, what was fake.

What was the truth, what was the lie?

She fumbled for the cord and shut the blinds, realizing she was only left with "why?"

FORTUNATELY, Robin didn't have to spend the evening pondering these questions about Johnny because an hour after Johnny left, Suzanne called, saying she was in the neighborhood, and could she drop off the laptop and discuss the speech contract tonight?

A blessing in disguise, Robin decided, because Suzanne's visit would give Robin something concrete to focus on instead of all the questions spinning in her mind about Johnny.

After Suzanne's phone call, Robin took off her pink Q-tip ensemble and threw on a pair of jeans and an old sweatshirt. Then she looked in the mirror and stifled a gasp. Her blond hair stuck out wildly all over her head. What she'd seen in her mind's eye as a sexily messy Elizabeth Hurly 'do actually looked as though Robin had put the blow-dryer on kill.

Yet Johnny had told her she looked hot, sexy. Either he loved bad hairdos, or he was a very good liar. Robin brushed her hair, wondering if that could really be true...was Johnny a good liar? By the time her hair was tame again, Robin heard a knock on the front door.

When she peeked through the peephole, a pair of pretty, sparkling hazel eyes were staring back. Suzanne.

"Nice to see you again," Suzanne said warmly as she strode in. Robin watched her, remembering her professor's confident gait as she'd paced casually in front of the class while lecturing. Not too many women could pull off a bravado attitude—but Suzanne did, and with finesse.

Suzanne looked around, one hand gripping the handle of a computer case, the other elegantly eased into the pocket of her khaki pants. "Shall I set up the laptop on your desk?"

Robin nodded, glad Suzanne was taking the initiative. Once she got the laptop up and running, and after Suzanne explained the assignment, Robin was certain she'd feel more comfortable speaking, asking questions.

On her way across the room, Suzanne eyed the table, next to Robin's recliner, with its scattered writing pads filled with cursive script. But Suzanne didn't ask any questions. Robin knew, though, that Suzanne saw Robin was actively writing and was probably pleased.

Minutes later, they were sitting at the desk. Robin sat on the backless, ergonomic rollaway chair. Suzanne sat perched on the desk, her arms crossed over her chest, explaining the assignment. "It's for a local corporation—OpticPower—have you read about them in the papers?"

Robin had been staring at the laptop, its monitor lit

with different icons, its electronics gently humming. She frowned. OpticPower. She'd read their ads for cell phone deals, read a few headlines about their stock rising or falling. "A-a little."

For the next ten minutes, Suzanne gave a brief lecture about OpticPower, explaining how the company started with several hundred employees five years ago and now boasted thirty-plus thousand. How OpticPower grew from a single product, fiber-optic telecommunications service, to an abundance of products, including cell phones, business software applications, Internet services.

"They've been the golden boy of the telecommunications industry...up to now," said Suzanne. "Recently, the media has hinted at some alleged illegalities in OpticPower's accounting practices. OpticPower's corporate communications department wants the CEO to give a speech that squashes the rumors once and for all."

Suzanne ran her fingers through her cropped, blond-streaked hair. "OpticPower's communications department contacted me because I taught several of the speechwriters who were once in the department, but it seems they've left for other jobs. And I don't want to write a speech because, as I explained to you on the phone, I love to *teach*, not do. But you, Robin, can do it." Suzanne smiled confidently, as though she believed Robin could move mountains if she put her mind to it. Seeing her former professor's belief in Robin almost took away the sting of being a dropout.

Suzanne cleared her throat. "Can I get a glass of water? I've been lecturing all day, and I'm starting to lose my voice." She grinned. "Some of my students might think that's a benefit."

Robin smiled, enjoying Suzanne's self-deprecating humor. Robin headed for the kitchen, planning to get the water and bring it back, but surprisingly Suzanne followed. It was odd to be walking around her tiny apartment with her former professor. It was almost as though they were girlfriends. Funny, after living alone for a solid year, Robin suddenly had *two* guests in these past few days. With a stab of yearning, Robin missed Buena Vista, her friends, her family.

After Suzanne drank some water, she looked around the kitchen. "Isn't this creative," she exclaimed.

Creative. The word took on new meaning—especially after last night's "creative" sex with Johnny. Turning her face so Suzanne wouldn't see heat filling her cheeks, Robin looked around, trying to see her kitchen as Suzanne did. She'd painted it a sunny yellow—mainly because the color was so cheery. Then she'd snipped pictures of food and recipes out of magazines and taped them to the outside of the kitchen cabinets, an act that seemed more logical than creative at the time. Robin loved food, loved writing—decorating her kitchen with pictures of food and recipes seemed natural. Eventually she'd decoupaged the clippings and recipes with an antiquing varnish, loving the atmospheric sheen it added to the kitchen.

Suzanne was fingering the metal basket that hung in

a corner next to the refrigerator. "It's like being in a market in Provence," Suzanne murmured.

Provence? Wasn't that in the south of France? Robin found herself shuffling her feet, unsure how to respond to a comment about her little south Denver kitchen being compared to the south of France.

Suzanne must have picked up on Robin's confusion, because Suzanne added, "The bright walls, the pictures on the cabinets, the vibrant colors of the fruits and vegetables displayed in these baskets..."

Robin looked at the baskets. Didn't everybody buy eggplant, tomatoes, bananas?

"You've picked out the best, most colorful, then you've displayed them like an artist." Suzanne looked at Robin and beamed her appreciation as though Robin was some kind of food Rembrandt. But before Robin could attempt a response, Suzanne suddenly gasped, holding both hands to her face as she spied something else. "And that adorable little house..." She crossed the room to a miniature hand-painted cottage that sat on the end of the kitchen counter. "It's so detailed and delicate."

It was one of her mother's hobbies, creating these small, whimsical cottages that she hand painted with great care, often customizing them for the recipients. She created one or two a month, giving them as gifts or selling them at a local crafts fair. For Robin, her mother had created a cottage to look like Emily's home in Amherst—along the outer walls was an excerpt from one of

Robin's favorite Dickinson poems, which Suzanne had just discovered.

"Oh!" Suzanne leaned closer, pulling a pair of reading glasses out of her blouse pocket. "There's a poem here." She read it out loud. "Hope is the thing with feathers, That perches in the soul, And sings the tune without the words, and never stops at all." She paused for a long moment. And when she looked at Robin, her eyes glistened. "That poem...it's like you," she whispered.

8

"IT'S LIKE ME?" Robin asked Mick, who was busy washing himself in the bowl of water she'd placed in his cage.

Robin yawned and took another sip of coffee, still touched that Suzanne thought the Dickinson poem was like Robin. Which part of the poem? Surely not the part about singing—because Suzanne wouldn't know that was the one verbal activity where Robin didn't stutter. Well, actually, she also didn't stutter when she was red-faced, spleen-bursting angry. But she rarely got that angry—nor would she want to be in order to be fluent. The last angry outburst she could recall had been years ago, the time she'd yelled at her brother for calling her the Pillsbury Dough Girl in that flouncy, chiffon dress her mother bought Robin to wear to the prom.

Her brother never, ever teased her about clothes, or anything else, after that. And Robin's mother had quietly exchanged the dress for something sleeker.

Robin took another sip of coffee, savoring its roasted flavor mixed with lots of milk. *No. Suzanne meant the part about "the tune without words."* And Robin was. That was probably the poem Robin had most identified with all her life because she felt Emily Dickinson *knew* what it was like to be quiet while a storm of emotions and thoughts raged inside. It had given Robin strength to know she wasn't alone—that someone else, well over a hundred years ago, had lived a similar existence.

Even with such an empathetic role model, Robin often thought it was unfortunate that there hadn't been a speech therapist at school when she was growing up. But Buena Vista had been so small, and the cost of seeing such a therapist wasn't covered by her mom's insurance. And, to be honest, at the time, the thought of meeting with some stranger and doing "talking" things had scared the bejesus out of Robin.

But lately, she'd been regretting not getting help with her stuttering. Maybe it was because of Johnny. He worked extra hard to find ways for them to communicate outside of words, and she appreciated his efforts, but it wasn't enough.

Because she *yearned* to talk to him.

She yearned to share everyday things with him. To tell him how her day had gone, tell him about getting this fab speech-writing assignment, tell him about her dreams and the books she'd read.

Maybe, if she'd had speech therapy, she wouldn't be a tune without words.

Robin glanced at the kitty clock—7:00 a.m. Yesterday, Robin had promised Suzanne a draft speech—or "talking points"—by this morning. Considering Robin needed two to three pages of bulleted items that the CEO would reference as he spoke, Robin had felt reasonably confident she could have something ready to review by this morning. She'd stayed up and played with ideas last night, and now Robin was eager to get back to work.

She'd listed Suzanne's instructions on a piece of paper, which she quickly reviewed again. Keep the tone professional, but light. Remind people that OpticPower used government-sanctioned accounting practices, the exact same as other telecommunications companies. And below, Robin had listed various computer operating instructions for starting the computer, reading e-mail, etc.

Two more cups of coffee later, Robin e-mailed the first draft of the speech to Suzanne for her review. Pumped with adrenaline and caffeine, Robin began pacing her living room, too anxious to sit and read or write. She passed the kitty clock and noted it was a little past nine. Suzanne said she'd be waiting for the first draft, so Robin hoped she'd hear from her soon. The sooner the better so Robin would have plenty of time to revise the speech before she had to get ready for work at 3:30.

After several pacing tours of the small room, she returned and stood at Mick's birdcage.

"Mick?" The bird remained staring at his image in the mirror, preoccupied. "Do you think Suzanne really meant 'she's like you' not 'it's like you'? You know, meant that Emily Dickinson is like me? Because no one could know *how* we're alike—quiet on the outside, wild on the inside. Most people think of Emily as a reclusive spinster, and I'm *not* like that." Just as Robin had been comfortable talking with her family, she was comfortable talking to Mick. Besides, that little comment of Suzanne's had been bothering Robin—she needed to talk to somebody about it!

Mick moved to hang upside down on a bar and Robin caught her reflection in the little shiny mirror in his cage. She laughed out loud. Her blond hair stuck out from her running her fingers through it repeatedly while writing and a smudge of chocolate streaked her cheek. And she was fretting about someone thinking she was a reclusive spinster? Right now she looked like a chocolate-dipped wild thing!

An artificially cheery voice interrupted her thoughts. "You've got mail!"

Robin blinked, then looked at the laptop monitor— sure enough, just as Suzanne had said, a little drawing of a mail truck appeared in the top right corner of the screen. Suzanne had written back *already!* Robin felt a mixture of curiosity and dread as she sat down at the computer. What if she'd written it all wrong? What if she had to start over from scratch?

Fortunately, Suzanne's revisions looked manageable. What surprised Robin most was Suzanne's request that Robin e-mail the second draft directly to the CEO himself. Robin absently reached for her mug and slugged a mouthful of cold coffee. Suzanne explained the CEO would be giving the speech earlier than originally scheduled—first thing tomorrow morning—so it simplified things for Robin to communicate directly with him.

Okay, Robin decided, it wasn't such a big deal to communicate with the CEO using e-mail. Just so long as Robin didn't have to speak with him on the phone.

But even more surprising was Suzanne's request at the end of the e-mail:

> Robin,
> OpticPower's communications department gave me the green light to farm out this job, but they asked me to submit all work, including any e-mails that document the CEO's revisions, under my account name to simplify bookkeeping. So in your communications with the CEO, please use my e-mail. Plus, this way, as you and I both have access to my e-mail account, I can track his requests and any additional revisions so you're paid appropriately.
>   You're doing a great job!
>   Best,
>   Suzanne

Send e-mail as Suzanne? A heaviness settled into Robin's chest. Submitting the draft to the CEO under Suzanne's name felt wrong, like lying, but after rereading the message several times, Robin decided if it was how the corporation wanted to handle it, then she should comply.

By noon, Robin was ready to transmit the new version directly to the CEO's e-mail address, jdp@opticpower.net. Still, she sat for a solid two minutes, the cursor hovering over the send button, debating if she should omit the word *robust* in a particular sentence. But she also knew she could keep changing and tweaking this speech for eternity, and time was of the essence. She smiled to herself. She wasn't a perfectionist until it came to words, then she weighed each one as though it was worth its weight in gold. That was the good part of being a stutterer. She probably valued words more than other people, and liked to take her time with them.

She clicked the send button.

Then she sat, she wasn't sure how many more minutes, just staring at the screen, amazed she'd completed this first real-world writing assignment.

And even more amazed when that strangely cheery "You've got mail!" voice talked to her again immediately!

Oh, God. What if it was a late-breaking message from Suzanne, who'd forgotten to give her an instruction? Or wanted Robin to add something before sending it...what if, what if...

Robin checked her e-mail and gulped a breath. It was a response from jdp@opticpower.net! Holy cow, when Suzanne said he was anxious for this speech, she wasn't kidding! Robin briskly rubbed her suddenly cold hands together before opening the e-mail and reading the message.

I'm not overly fond of the word *robust* so I'll substitute something else.

Otherwise, nice job!

Thanks.

Robin blinked and reread the message. *Nice job.* Mr. CEO liked it! Funny, he didn't sign his name. CEO types were probably too busy for such small, personal touches...after all, they had major corporations to run.

But he'd told her she'd done a "nice job." Robin felt elated over those two words—and kept repeating them to herself the rest of the afternoon, even as she got ready for work and headed to Davey's Diner for the evening shift.

"HOT STUFF, how you gettin' home?" It was nearing midnight. Al had finished cleaning the grill and setting up the cooking area for the morning cook's breakfast shift.

Robin looked around to see who Al was calling "hot stuff." Dottie was in the back room, smoking a cigarette while chatting on the pay phone to a girlfriend, so it appeared Robin's nickname was officially "Hot Stuff."

"Walking," she said softly, reaching for her sweater. She'd finished her chores and was ready to go home.

"At this hour?" Al grunted his disapproval. "Dottie and I will drive you."

Dottie and I. So they really were an item. Feelings of longing filled Robin as she recalled how great it had felt when Johnny had waited for her, walked her home. But those feelings turned bittersweet as questions remained unanswered, questions she wished she'd been able to ask. Such as why Johnny never had a car. She'd just assumed when he said he took the light-rail that he was on a tight budget, like herself, and that he relied on public transportation. But people on tight budgets didn't take limos. And realizing Johnny was hiding something from her undermined her most important value in the world. *Truth.*

"Dottie Doll," Al called out, "hang up. We're driving Robin home."

Robin wondered if Al saw the mixed emotions on Robin's face because he was looking at her all sadlike. She didn't know if she could handle Al going sensitive on her. Yet in the last few days she was starting to realize he had a heart as big as his body. A gruff heart, like its master, but a big heart all the same.

Minutes later, Robin was sitting in the front seat of the green pickup, with Al behind the wheel and Dottie squeezed in the middle. Robin noticed how Al occasionally patted Dottie on her leg or tweaked her cheek. And how Dottie snuggled tight against him. Robin never would have dreamed these two would fall for each other—but then she'd never dreamed that Johnny Dayton would come back into her life, either.

Al turned the ignition, several times, until finally the engine chugged to life. He fussed with the radio, turning the dial until he found a country station. Some male singer was crooning about the cheatin' side of town.

"Where to?" Al said loudly, glancing over at Robin.

She winced. She hated talking and here she was being forced to not only talk, but loud enough to be heard over a cranky engine and a country song!

Dottie nudged her elbow into Al's side. "Ladies don't yell," she yelled, and Robin had to quickly look away so nobody caught her smiling. Dottie was skinny, but had an attitude bigger than Al's body. Dottie was also the penultimate "girlfriend"—if any of her gal pals needed a caring ear, they first called Dottie. And the way Dottie talked and kidded and checked up on Robin these last few days, Robin realized she'd become one of Dottie's gal pals.

Dottie tweaked the volume and the male crooner grew softer. Gently touching Robin's arm, Dottie asked, "Where to, honey bun?"

Between the two of them, Robin had more sweet-talking names than she'd ever had in her life! Hot stuff. Honey bun. Where'd they get these endearments? Al was keeping mum about Robin's little tabletop melt-down the other night, but if he ever called her "Coffee Clutch," at least she'd know why.

Robin gave the directions, simply with minimal words, and Al nodded. Then they were off.

As they drove the few blocks to her place, the only sounds in the cab were the rumbling engine and turned-up crooning singer...until Al again spoke.

"Where's that boyfriend of yours?"

Robin thought her insides had turned to ice. The question took her by surprise—she wasn't aware Al had seen Johnny waiting to walk her home these past few nights. But even if she had the gift of gab, and could talk fluently and endlessly, the last topic she wanted to discuss was Johnny and his business trip. She had so many questions about it herself, she just didn't know what was real and what wasn't.

Dottie nudged Al in the ribs again. "None of your damn business." Then she turned to Robin and touched her lightly on the arm again. "Where is he, honey?"

So the two of them had even discussed her relationship with Johnny! But Robin didn't feel awkward about it—in fact, Dottie's obvious concern warmed some of the cold trickling through Robin's veins. "B-business," she answered, clueless as to what that business really was.

"He helpin' you out with your car?" Al barked.

Yep, Al was mad. Robin rarely heard this angry tone unless a customer complained too much about his cooking—Robin had once seen Al, after having to recook an order twice, march out into the dining room and serve the customer himself. Robin hadn't really heard what Al said to the customer, but the guy ate his food quietly and left. And never returned.

This time Dottie sighed loudly. "You're nosier than my Aunt Clarisse, Al honey."

Robin waited for Dottie to turn and repeat the question to her, as though nosiness was a given between gal pals, but Dottie didn't. Instead, she tapped her foot in time to the music, humming along. Dottie was sharp. She knew bits and pieces about the towed car, knew Robin had dropped out of school, but she also knew not to pry too much. Probably also knew Robin would stutter, big time, if she was pressured to answer overly sensitive questions.

After Al pulled the truck up in front of her apartment building, Robin turned to the two of them. Stray light from an overhead streetlamp offered little illumination in the cab, but enough for Robin to see that Al and Dottie looked worried.

"I—I'm okay," Robin said, hoping the simple statement would take away that look in their eyes. It didn't. They were sweet, fretting about Robin's personal life. If the three of them kept up this camaraderie, even Al would become her gal pal. Smiling at the thought, Robin opened the truck's passenger door and hopped out.

Five minutes later, after she'd doffed her rayon work outfit, smeared and dotted with grease, relish and some orange streaks that were either from carrots or oranges, she threw on one of her long T-shirts and meandered into the kitchen to get Mick's dinner. Grabbing some grapes, and the bag of seeds, she headed to his cage...and stopped in her tracks.

She'd forgotten to turn off the laptop and there it was, monitor emitting ghostly rays into the darkened room, with that little mail truck prominently displayed in the top right of the screen. Someone had either sent her, or Suzanne, an e-mail.

Robin plunked the grapes and seeds into Mick's bowl, then headed straight to the desk, sat down, and opened the e-mail program. If a message was obviously for the "real" Suzanne, Robin would ignore it. But she should check.

The e-mail was from jpd@opticpower.net.

If Robin's tummy felt icy earlier, it felt like a blizzard raging inside her now. *Maybe the CEO's changed his mind—gone from "nice job" to "I hate it!" Or maybe he's decided he not only dislikes the word* robust, *he's now wanting new words for* synergy *and* global growth *and—God forbid—*accounting. *What in the world is another word for* accounting? Robin put her hands over her eyes, not wanting to look at the message. *If Mom were here, she'd tell me to stop overreacting and just read the message.*

Robin lowered her hands and read jpd's message.

After tomorrow morning's speech, I'm heading to a local university to meet some new college hires. I need some talking points. This group is mainly computer-science graduates, but I'd like to appeal to them, not just their technical studies.

Can you help?

Busy guy, no sign-off signature again, Robin noted. She also noted he'd written around 11:00 p.m., making it a *very* last-minute request, so she could feel comfortable saying that, unfortunately, she didn't have time to help.

But his request also appealed to Robin on multiple levels. He wanted talking points that would relate to college kids? This guy was talking to Ms. Current College Student herself! Well, Ms. Former Current, anyway. Plus, the extra job meant extra money and she could get her car out of hock sooner....

She wrote back.

I can help. I'll forward you some ideas in a few minutes.

She didn't sign off with any name, just as he hadn't. Plus, she would have felt weird writing *Suzanne* at the end of her message.

Then she leaned back in her chair and thought about what she might have liked to hear if a big CEO visited one of her classrooms. What might a telecommunications CEO say to her that would make her feel he was reaching out to *her* and not just any audience?

She jotted down some notes on her notepad, references to hot bands that were experimenting with digital sounds—jpd could segue into how his company was marketing digital devices, how students use wireless phones—jpd might reveal new plans OpticPower has for wireless products, plus a quote from Dave Matthews on technology. She toyed with looking up something that Mick Jagger might have said about technology—after all, Mick was her favorite performer—but he was getting a little old. She opted to use the Dave Matthews quote, although she bet jpd wouldn't have a clue who she meant.

She e-mailed her notes.

Within minutes, she heard, "You've got mail!"

Already? Didn't that guy do anything but work?

Great job.

Thanks.

P.S. Who's Dave Matthews?

Yep, he's clueless. But before writing back, she reveled in the second, and even better, compliment. "Great job." Wow. Here she was sitting in her jammies, writing stuff for a CEO, who said she was doing a great job. This was almost as good as winning that writing award in middle school.

She wrote back, describing the Dave Matthews Band, their popularity and how they'd even had an ice cream named after them. To her surprise, the CEO wrote back quickly, commenting how his taste in music ran more to classical. She thought maybe she shouldn't write back again. After all, this was a very busy and important man who had better things to do than send e-mail messages about music and ice cream. But it felt so good to be "conversing" fluently, even if it was in written messages. This was something she never got to share with anyone, even Johnny.

Johnny. He had said he'd call, let the phone ring twice, but if she was online, using the only phone line in her place, he couldn't very well "ring twice." And she had a phone machine, not a messaging service, so he'd just get a busy signal. She felt a twinge of guilt, but she also felt other emotions. Hurt, confusion. She felt torn apart with all her questions about his possible deceit. And if she got off the computer just to sit in the dark and wait for the phone to ring, she'd feel even more up-set...especially if the phone didn't ring.

As these thoughts ran amok in her mind, another e-mail popped up.

You write speeches, so you must write other things. Like what?

She hesitated, pausing before she wrote back. Maybe she should ask him a question, too.

I write short stories.
   Who do you like to read?

She hit the send button. This was becoming more and more like a conversation.

And so began a series of e-mails where he said he used to read fiction, but that it was a luxury he didn't have time for these days. When she asked what he used to read, he wrote:

Heroic fantasies. But now, with reading all of the papers and reports required by work, the last thing I want to do is read when I get home, so my great escape is music. Beethoven when I'm moody, Mo-zart when I've had a good day.

But Robin, the lover of words, wanted to know more about these "heroic fantasies." Why that particular kind? He'd written back a one-line response "because they helped me overcome my problems at home," then he asked her what she liked to read.

Obviously, he didn't want to explain more about his reading choices, so she wrote about reading a variety of books, but mostly she enjoyed reading poetry. Without realizing it, Robin's fingers were flying across the keyboard as she wrote about the poems of Browning, Frost, Dickinson. It was as though Robin was doing more than opening up a dialogue—she was opening her heart, revealing her deepest passions.

When she realized it was one in the morning, she politely mentioned it was late, although secretly, she hated to sign off. It had felt fantastic to "talk" freely. This conversation with the CEO had been one of those serendipity things, something out of the blue, yet it had rocked Robin's world. She'd drop Suzanne an e-mail to let her know about tonight's e-mail exchanges so Suzanne wouldn't be taken aback—after all, Suzanne had access to all the exchanges Robin had with jpd. If there was a professional problem communicating with the CEO this way, Suzanne could let Robin know. But Robin doubted there would be. Surely, people in business sometimes talked informally—wasn't that part of building good client relations?

After she logged off and laid out her sleeping bag, she contemplated how Dickinson, in her reclusive lifestyle, was also greatly affected by chance encounters. How from brief interactions, she'd write powerful poetry—indicative of the depths to which a near stranger could move her world.

Sort of like Robin's interaction with jpd tonight.

Looking up at the Colorado night sky through her window, Robin wished she and Johnny shared such conversations, but then, that was her fault. When she thought of it, the most meaningful verbal connection she'd ever had with Johnny was years ago, when as a kid she'd whispered "thank you" to him as she stood at the podium, receiving her award.

Robin reflected on the wealth of words she'd exchanged tonight with the CEO. She bet if she told her mom what had happened tonight, and how profound it felt, her mom would say it was one of those "the universe is telling you something" experiences.

"Thank you," she whispered to the vast sky, hoping the universe told her something again, soon.

Two thousand miles away in Newport, Rhode Island, Johnny stood on the balcony of his hotel room, looking over the scenic harbor front. It was late, after three in the morning, but he was wide-awake. He picked a single twinkling light out of the star-splattered sky, and pondered the odds of two total strangers, out of millions of people, enjoying a spontaneous late-night conversation.

Although he felt a bit guilty for the extensive e-mail correspondence he'd had tonight with Suzanne. They hadn't flirted, he justified to himself. It had merely been a lively, intellectual conversation. Yet...to be honest with himself, it had been intimate. *Emotionally* intimate. Suzanne's words had been filled with so much passion and exuberance, he could almost feel her emotions radiating off the computer screen. Hardly what he expected from a casual e-mail exchange with a contracted speechwriter.

He supposed he felt guilty because he'd encouraged their e-mails, but it was the first time in he didn't know how long, that he'd enjoyed a comfortable, in-depth conversation with someone who wasn't focused on business. His staff and employees seemed more interested in saying the right thing and pleasing him than speaking their minds. And as for the women in his past, well, if he heard one more story about shopping in Cherry Creek, honest to God, he'd set fire to that district of Denver.

But Suzanne had been different. She talked about music, literature, that Dave Matthews Band. He'd have to listen to them—Suzanne had peaked his interest talking about their organic style and early grassroots success. The latter, especially, because he knew how it felt to build a business from scratch.

And he'd told her something he'd never shared with anyone—how, growing up, he escaped his home life by reading heroic fantasies. In his mind's eye, he could see himself in the corner of the living room, a blanket over his head, reading by flashlight. It had been like a special world he created, an escape from the reality just an arm's length away. During summer, when he wasn't working, he had a favorite spot down by the creek where he'd sit, lean against a cottonwood and read with only rushing water and chirping birds in the background.

He hadn't written Suzanne about his corner of the living room or the creek, but he did tell her how the bigger-than-life heroes made his problems seem smaller, more manageable. How he'd especially admired Agamemnon because, hell, if *that* guy could face the curse of the house of Pelops, Johnny could certainly face handling a delinquent brother and a drunken father.

He'd never discussed such things with Robin. Their intimacies were physical, spiritual even, but for the first time, he ached to share *words* with her. At least he'd tried to call her tonight. The hotel room had several phone lines, so while writing Suzanne, he'd tried phoning Robin but always got a busy signal. He'd thought it odd that Robin would be on the phone for so long. Had to have been someone in her family—someone she felt comfortable talking with.

Maybe she'd be that comfortable with him someday. Maybe.

He stepped back into the hotel room, hoping he didn't fall asleep with all the lights on as he finished reading his business reports.

THE NEXT DAY, his speeches went well. In between meetings, he phoned Robin, using his two-ring code. Both times she answered, but the conversations had been one-sided, which Johnny reminded himself was okay. After all, he'd told her she didn't have to speak.

But that night, sitting in his hotel room again, the

loneliness crowded him to the point he thought he'd go mad if he didn't connect with life, somehow. The conversations with Suzanne last night had resurrected why he'd left his childhood home. Resurrected the pain of not being able to protect his family.

Resurrected things he never talked about. But tonight, he thought about them...again.

It had been the night before he left for college. Frankie had had another brush with the law. His father, emboldened with booze, had lashed out, accusing Johnny of not protecting his little brother. Johnny was accustomed to his father's drunken rants, but this night, his father sucker punched Johnny. Lying on the floor, his mouth bleeding, Johnny realized he'd never be able to save his family. He'd always be a failure. That was the night he left Buena Vista, never to return...

...except for occasional drives to his father's grave. He'd had a lot of one-sided conversations with that tombstone during the past few years.

He flipped open the laptop, not wanting to be alone again tonight. This wasn't being unfaithful to Robin, it was needing an honest, real conversation. He didn't want to delve into his past—he just wanted simple companionship. He wanted words.

He brought up his e-mail program and filled in Suzanne's address....

9

ROBIN WAS HUMMING a Dave Matthews tune, wondering if it had any hidden "heroic fantasy" meaning. This was jpd's fault. Jpd. Shoot, she'd meant to ask his first name, but the e-mails had been so swift and lively the past few nights, it had been all she could do to keep up with the topics. She especially liked how he'd surprised her—well not *her* really, but her as *Suzanne*—late last night. He'd just wanted to write, to "talk," and talk they did. What she found most interesting was that comment he'd made about Agamemnon, and how Agamemnon should never have returned home. She'd asked him what that meant, and he'd written back about having a tough home life growing up—a life where he'd been unable to protect his family. Then he'd added that he always kept an African mask on his desk that symbolized the protector and healer...and how it was his reminder of what he'd failed to do and what he still wanted to do.

She'd sensed he didn't want to discuss that aspect of his life anymore, so she casually mentioned that although she hadn't had a tough home life, she certainly related to "tough times" growing up. But she didn't go into particulars, mainly because she didn't want to confess her tough times were due to being a stutterer. It had been too wonderful to simply "talk" to someone and be free with words, even if they were typed ones.

It had felt so yin and yang with jpd, as though they were two pieces that fit. Intellectually, of course. Anything more, anything *flirtatious,* would be wrong. After all, she was still dating Johnny. She felt confused whenever she thought of him, but there was nothing she could do about it on her own. She'd have to see him, find a way to tell him what was on her mind, see how he responded.

She glanced at the clock—3:20 p.m. Almost time to shower, get ready for work.

Knock, knock.

She headed to the peephole and peered through it.

There were those familiar blue eyes looking back at her. *Johnny.* Her insides did funny things as she caught her breath. Was she ready to see him? She felt so confused about his guardedness, his clothes, that limo. But despite everything, the fact was, deep down, he was still Johnny Dayton. The guy who sat in the front row at her middle-school award ceremony, cheering her on. The guy she'd spent years daydreaming about, fantasizing over. Yes, something was wrong with the current picture, but he'd proven his goodness and loyalty in the past. She rolled back her shoulders and put her hand on the doorknob. Things weren't right, but it was only fair he be given a chance to explain. She opened the door and stepped back.

When he stepped inside, she felt as though they'd

gone back in time. There stood the Johnny from years ago. Well-worn pair of jeans, a plain white T-shirt visible above a crinkled black leather jacket that matched his raven hair. He looked tired, but those blue eyes bore into her with that familiar intensity. For a fleeting moment, she felt like the twelve-year-old girl in the park, being rescued by her hero, Johnny Dayton.

He smiled, and her heart melted at the warmth in his face. He looked so happy—relieved, even—to see her.

"How's my girl?" he asked huskily.

"Fine," she mouthed. She'd wanted to speak, probably could have spoken, but didn't have the breath to form the words. His gaze traveled slowly over her, and she swore she heard her pounding heart echoing against the walls.

"You certainly look fine," he said suggestively.

She glanced down at her long pink T-shirt and realized her hardened nipples were pressing through the thin fabric. Well, he obviously didn't need her to tell him how she felt about him—her body was speaking loudly for her! Suddenly, she didn't care about her questions and confusions. *Whatever is going on in his life, I know his heart is Johnny's. That's all that matters right now.*

As their gazes held for a long moment, she imagined if she were more comfortable speaking, what she'd say to him. *I saw the limo, Johnny. I'm not very sophisticated, but I know an expensive suit when I see one...and that gold watch. Maybe I'm a tune without words, but are you a tune with lies? Johnny, explain the false notes I'm hearing.*

The thoughts subsided as she became acutely aware of his presence, his scent. Masculine, freshly showered.

Shower! Work!

"I..." Without breaking their locked gaze, she pointed absently over her shoulder at the clock.

He followed her motion. "It's almost three-thirty." He looked back into her eyes, searching them. "Time for you to get ready for work?"

She nodded.

"Don't let me stop you."

A few minutes later, she stepped into the shower, fighting the disappointment that he hadn't stopped her. Right there, next to the door, on the floor. She let the warm water sluice over her naked body as she closed her eyes, wondering if she should turn the water colder to shake her out of her hot thoughts, help her focus on getting ready for work.

Johnny paced in the living room, back and forth, giving the orange pillow a slight kick as he passed it. He was pent-up, hot, especially after seeing sweet Robin in that body-hugging pink number. Those breasts, full and puckered, had told him what she was thinking...what she was needing...

And he needed it, too. Bad.

He stopped and stared out the window, remembering the other night. How it'd felt to touch her, kiss her, their give-and-take love play. Back in Buena Vista, when she was a kid, he'd seen that mischievous, playful side of her. As a woman, her playfulness had a sexy edge. God, just thinking about her was putting *him* on edge.

Mick chirped and Johnny shot him a sideways glance. "Your owner is one hot lady." Mick fluttered and chirped in response. That, and the sound of water spray in the background blended into a sensuous mix of sounds that wrapped around him, enticing him.

And then he heard Robin singing.

Her voice was soft and sweet as it half hummed, half sang an unrecognizable tune, her gentle crooning blending with the hush of water. It was like a drug, listening to her singing, the gift of her voice he so rarely heard. Johnny felt like an Argonaut on a ship, lured by the song of the Sirens. He flashed on her shower curtain—decorated with wildly colored birds—and recalled how the ancients often depicted the Sirens as having the bodies of birds and the heads of women.

Her light, melodic voice teased the air, mingling with the intoxicating scents from the bouquet, weaving a spell around him. Drawing him to her...

If he'd been lashed to a post, as Odysseus had been, he might have been able to stop himself. But the lure of her voice was more than he could bear. Driven by a force beyond his will, he began walking toward the bathroom, pulling off his jacket.

ROBIN RUBBED the bar of soap over her body, inhaling its fragrance of wild rose. This French-milled soap was her single indulgence. She didn't have a TV, hadn't bought a new dress in she didn't know how long, but whenever she had a few extra dollars, she splurged on a bar of this soap. She loved its creamy texture and how it produced the frothiest bubbles as she rubbed it over her skin. She was humming fragments of an old love song, singing the words she remembered, humming the rest.

At some point, she realized another hand was massaging soap into her skin, and she gasped. Turning slightly, she saw Johnny, standing outside the tub where he held back the curtain with one hand while the other massaged and rubbed her. He wore only his jeans, just as he had the other night, his bare chest a chiseled mass of muscle and hair. She was stunned by his presence, excited by how his hand kept moving over her body, massaging her breasts, thighs and teasingly skirting the tendrils between her legs.

Then he withdrew his hand. Without a word, he popped the top button on his jeans. He paused, watching her reaction, as though asking what she wanted.

"More," she whispered, riveted by the visual show he was giving her. God help her, she wanted to see him, *all* of him.

He pulled down the zipper of his pants, and tugged down his jeans. He pulled each jean leg over his bare feet.

She stared at his crotch. She couldn't stop herself. It bulged magnificently through a pair of tight, black briefs. She clasped the bar of soap between her hands to stop herself from stepping out of this tub and yanking those sexy black undies down herself. But, no. She wanted to see what he did because he wasn't simply undressing...he was *teasing* her. Her body responded, trembling with arousal.

He held his pants midair and reached into a pocket, extracting a small square packet. *A condom.* He winked at her before tossing his pants aside. Knowing he'd planned ahead excited her—although she sensed his decision to invade her shower had been a very spontaneous act. He gently placed the packet on the edge of the tub. Standing, he hitched one thumb inside the elastic band of his briefs.

She waited.

He pulled it down a little, exposing a mass of curly black hair.

She waited.

So did he.

She was having trouble breathing, but managed to whisper again, "More."

His lips pulled back in a wicked grin and he pulled them down a bit more...then all the way down, stepping out of them. Then he stood, naked outside the shower, observing her watching him.

"Wow."

He chuckled as he tossed the black briefs on top of his jeans. "Well, when you speak up, you certainly choose the appropriate moment."

She wanted to say more, how in all her fantasies, she'd never, ever imagined him to be so...so...*impressive.*

He stepped into the shower and pulled the curtain closed. "Turn around," he said.

She turned her back to him. As the warm water sprayed across her breasts, she felt him ease the bar of soap from her hand. He rubbed it along her shoulders, slid it along her arms, and trailed it all the way across her back. His movements were careful, scrupulous, as though he were bathing a precious object. When he reached her bottom, he rolled the soap in slow, lazy circles on each cheek before dipping it between her legs.

Heat infused her, filling her with need. She moaned and leaned her palms against the cool tile, letting the warm water tickle down her hardening nipples. She spread her legs a little, relishing the increased motion of his hand, hot and creamy with soap, between her legs.

His hands then slid back up to her waist, and gently he turned her around to face him. Her heart quickened as their bodies pressed against each other—warm, soapy skin against skin. She pressed her face against his chest and burrowed her lips into his silky chest hair to kiss his chest. He tasted like salt and man, water and heat. She ran her hands over his body, memorizing its terrain, its wonder.

When she raised her head, he pulled her tighter against him and she gasped at the sheer pleasure of feeling their bodies molded together. It was almost as though they were one, the way they fit. Curves pressed into muscle, softness contoured to solidity. Two parts of a whole.

Sheets of water sluiced over them, like a waterfall. The overhead light poured through the colored birds on the shower curtain, cascading colors—vivid reds, blues, greens—over their wet bodies. It was as though they were in an exotic land, their very own private world, filled with dreamlike colors and the hypnotic hush of water. A world where words weren't necessary because their bodies communicated their desire and need for each other. As if to prove it, she caught a look in Johnny's eyes, bluer than the azure that streamed through the curtain, and saw he knew her in a way no one else knew her.

Just as she knew him. Despite everything, whatever his small deceits, she knew the real Johnny.

As their gazes locked, she felt her heart reach out to him, pouring love with more force than the water streaming over them. Maybe earlier she'd had her doubts about his life, but at this moment there was no doubt in her mind that the man in her arms was Johnny, the true Johnny, the man of her dreams, the only man she'd ever desired...

...and even more, the only man she would ever truly love.

She held him closer, wanting to burn this moment into her brain, into her soul, so she could keep it always. She knew better than anyone else that the present didn't promise the future, that events could change in the blink of an eye, but she'd always have this memory no matter what.

Johnny lowered his hands to her buttocks and pressed her against his groin. When she moaned, letting her head fall back, with that open look of pure passion on her sweet face, it was all he could do to hold himself

back. Especially when her body melted into his, opening herself to him.

He ground his pelvis against her, aware of her trembling, her moaning, the rush of water. She was like a Siren the way her voice moaned, beckoned to him. And
he was like a doomed sailor in the heroic-fantasy tale,
so inextricably drawn to her, so mesmerized by her, he
would willingly die to own her.

It had never been like this with a woman. Never. The
colors, the rush of water, the intense need. He found her
lips, which stilled under his for a heartbeat. Then he felt
them move. "Johnny," she murmured. "You're my
Johnny."

And at that moment, his guard slipped away. Like
silt washed away by the water...and a woman's love.

Robin heard herself speak his name. Her words had
been fluent, effortless. It told her how perfect this moment was, how right. When his fingers trailed up the inside of her thighs, arousal spiraled within her. Reaching
down, she pulled his hand onto her mons as, with her
other hand, she gripped his shaft. The real world spun
away as they caressed and teased each other. Repeatedly, his touch brought her to the edge of orgasm, causing her to whimper with need as she succumbed to the
exquisite torture. Her body was on fire, her nerves
ablaze.

"Now," she whispered between urgent gasps.

Johnny reached down, ripped open the wrapper, and
sheathed himself. She stood, her nipples arched and
hard, panting, waiting. He meant to take it slow,

wanted to take it slow, but the heat, her voluptuous body slick with water and soap, drove him with a hot urgency. He lifted her, enough to edge inside her opening. Holding his breath, he entered her. A cry escaped her lips, which he caught with a kiss as he sank deep inside her. He pumped slowly at first, carefully withdrawing his shaft before sliding into her again. When her pelvis moved with his rhythm, he thrust deeper, again and again, while his tongue plundered her mouth.

When her insides convulsed she sobbed, crying his name, over and over. He responded with a low groan that built in intensity until he exploded within her.

Johnny's head dropped onto her chest as he panted, releasing the tension. Her words echoed in his mind. *Johnny. You're my Johnny.* He was grateful for the rushing water because it hid the sting of moisture in his eyes. Wrapping his arms around Robin, he held her tight like a dream from which he didn't want to awaken, thanking her silently for giving him back himself.

"I'M OKAY," Robin said to Dottie and Al, who once again had that combined worried look like two fretting parents. With a smile, Robin slammed shut the pickup passenger door, wishing these two lovebirds would worry about something else.

As she dashed up the steps to her apartment, she wished she could have told them that everything was okay, despite appearances. True, Johnny hadn't been there to walk her home again tonight, but after they'd made love this afternoon, he'd explained he had a lot on his plate after his business trip. He needed to take care of his own home—mail, phone messages—tasks that had piled up after being out of town. He'd walked her to work and lingered with her outside the front door to Davey's Diner. He'd even tried to give her money for a taxi, but at that moment Dottie had sauntered into work, asking loudly whether Robin would need a ride home again, so Johnny had realized Robin had safe transportation home.

After a lingering kiss, which Al and Dottie witnessed, no doubt, Johnny told Robin he'd call her later.

Opening the door to her apartment, Robin sighed, remembering this afternoon in the shower...how she and Johnny had made intoxicating, fantastic, mesmerizing love. And no way was Robin being overdramatic about that! Afterward, when Johnny had walked her to work, she didn't want to break the spell by asking him the questions that bothered her. She'd ask later when their minds were cool and before their bodies got hot again.

"Hi, Mick," she called out, walking toward the kitchen. "Fruit and seeds are on their way." She returned with some slices of apple and placed them in his food bowl. Then she glanced at the laptop on her desk, hidden underneath some papers and books. She needed to drop Suzanne an e-mail, let her know she could pick up her computer.

Moments later, Robin had logged on. The "You've Got Mail!" voice greeted her. She checked—from Suzanne to Suzanne, with the subject line "Robin, read this."

Robin opened the e-mail message.

Robin,
Urgent request: OpticPower wants another speech. CEO is giving statement to media, 11:00 a.m. tomorrow, at OpticPower main office. See attached article from the *Denver Post*.

Seems a woman in Wyoming claims OpticPower service workers accidentally severed cable lines, preventing her from calling 9-1-1 to get emergency help for her son who was hurt in an accident. The son survived, thank God, but she's blaming OpticPower for her child almost dying. Optic-Power claims no responsibility, and their CEO wants to address the media immediately. Can you draft something tonight? OpticPower will pay extra due to this rush turnaround.

Please send your draft directly to jpd@opticpower.net. Got fantastic feedback on your last two writing projects, so your working directly with the CEO works well.

Regards,

Suzanne

Robin read the article. A young mother, who lived on a small ranch outside Laramie, Wyoming told the media her two-year-old son had been seriously injured in a fall from a tractor. She'd tried to dial 9-1-1, but there was no dial tone on her phone line. She drove her son forty miles to the nearest hospital emergency room, where they managed to save her son's life. Hospital sources claimed, however, that if she'd been any later, her son would have died.

Robin's heart pounded while reading the story. In some ways, it reminded her of her mother's accident seven years ago. There were three people, she and her mother in one car—the kid who ran the stop sign in the truck. Her mother had been fighting for consciousness and no one had a cell phone. She knew how that young mother must have felt to be in a crisis with no phone access. For Robin, however, a passing driver pulled over, had a cell and called an ambulance. That poor young mother in Laramie had no choice but to drive her injured child miles to the hospital, hoping he didn't die before she got help.

But what was especially eerie about the two stories was that the young mother in Wyoming and Robin's mother were both fighting for the truth. It seemed that way to Robin, anyhow. The young mother appeared to be adamant that OpticPower was at fault—and if that was the case, the corporation owed her, at minimum, to be honest about their mistake. A blank "it wasn't our fault" reminded Robin of the kid's lie at her mother's trial.

Tears filled her eyes and the computer screen blurred. *I can't write a speech about OpticPower's innocence without knowing the truth. I'll get that young mother's number, ask her questions.* Robin crossed to the phone on the side table next to the recliner and stared at the numbered buttons.

Call? Speak to a total stranger?

She eased out a long, slow breath. *This is important. Just pick up the phone and dial Information.* She picked up the receiver and punched in the numbers for Information. When the automated response system asked what city she was calling, Robin said "Laramie" fluently. When asked what state, she said, "Wy-Wy-Wy-Wy—" It was like being stuck, endlessly, not knowing when the verbal glitch would end....

"Wy-Wy—"

Frustrated, she hung up. Then dropped her head into her hands and wished she could cry.

No.

She raised her head and looked out at the Colorado sky. The sky she shared with Buena Vista, the sky she always wondered if her mom was looking up at, maybe sharing the same view with her daughter.

Robin smiled. *I'll call Mom. Ask her to be my researcher.* Reaching for the phone, Robin decided maybe the universe was sending signals all the time...and Robin had just caught another one.

JOHNNY SAT in his den, sipping a cognac, listening to Beethoven's Pastoral Symphony. Outside the window, the night was dark, overcast, like the music. And his mood. Hard to believe not so many hours ago he'd made love to Robin and felt on top of the world. Then he'd come home, where William informed him Optic-

Power's legal counsel had been leaving urgent messages for Mr. Dayton to call, immediately.

Johnny had spent the rest of afternoon and into the evening with his legal counsel, discussing the Wyoming mother's accusations against OpticPower. Johnny had been through similar events, but never one where a citizen's complaint made OpticPower look like an evil monster. Johnny had demanded an investigation into her accusations, which his lawyer claimed had been done. OpticPower, the lawyer had stated emphatically, was not at fault because there had been no OpticPower service truck within a twenty-mile radius of the location where the cable had been cut. "What you're dealing with," his legal counsel claimed, "is a poor single mother who sees an opportunity to make lots of money by suing OpticPower. She views us as a cash cow."

But everywhere Johnny looked, at the TV, in the papers, he saw that young mother's face, tears streaming down her face, not only claiming her son almost died due to OpticPower's negligence, but that she had a witness that OpticPower severed the cable.

"Some boy on drugs," the lawyer had scoffed. "Kid has a history of thefts, brushes with the law. Unreliable witness."

Johnny had thought of his kid brother, Frankie. Maybe if Johnny had believed in his brother more, helped him more, Frankie wouldn't have ended up in jail. Johnny stuffed the thought back into the past, the place where he could never return and fix things.

"It's imperative you make a statement to the media,"

his lawyer had said. Johnny agreed. The local news stations had been calling, hounding him for a comment, and Johnny agreed he'd meet with them outside OpticPower's offices tomorrow morning, 11:00 a.m., to give a statement. He and the lawyer agreed on the key points Johnny would make, and Johnny had placed an urgent request with his communications manager for a speech. "I want Suzanne," he'd instructed. "She works fast, nails the spin and knows my tone."

"Another cognac, Mr. Dayton?"

Johnny looked over at William, who stood in the doorway, wearing a pair of black satin pajamas, holding that day's paper under his arm. He'd probably been picking dogs in tomorrow's races. Johnny smiled, welcoming the interruption.

"You know I never have more than one drink." And Johnny knew that William was just looking for an excuse to come downstairs and talk. Worrying about Johnny again, no doubt.

William blinked. "I read the papers."

"Join the club." Jonathan looked at his glass, catching a spark of reddish light reflecting off the crystal snifter. It reminded him of the spilling colors through the shower curtain as he and Robin had made love. He released a weighty sigh. Except for the magical time spent with Robin, it had been a hellishly long day. He needed to check his computer, see if the drafted speech was ready, and fine-tune it. It was going to be a long night, preparing for tomorrow's media pit bulls who smelled blood and were ready for the kill.

"William," he said, cocking his head, "I'm going to the dogs tomorrow."

"Pardon, sir?"

"The media dogs, not the racing ones." He killed the rest of the cognac, then stood. He needed a reprieve from the day's stress. A moment to talk about anything but accusations, potential lawsuits. "Did you visit the dog races while I was out of town?"

William's faded blue eyes twinkled. "Pretty Lady made them eat her dust," he said proudly.

Johnny smiled to himself, thinking of another pretty, and older, lady. "I, uh, would like you to take one of my colleagues to the races soon."

"Colleague?"

Jonathan crossed the room, stopping in front of William. "Yes, a colleague. I think you two—I mean, I think you would be an excellent...tour guide for my colleague."

William blinked, obviously taken aback. "Tour guide?"

Good Lord, he had that same tone Shelia had had when Jonathan made the suggestion. He'd never met two people more alike—set in their ways, exasperatingly organized and needing to take care of someone other than themselves. *They're perfect for each other.*

"Yes, a tour. My treat. First, take my colleague to lunch at the country club—order a bottle of the best champagne—then give a tour of the dog races. How to pick a dog, place a bet, that sort of thing."

William looked at Johnny as though he'd lost a few marbles. "I'll make arrangements, Mr. Dayton."

"Good." Johnny started to walk toward his bedroom, but paused.

"And William?"

"Yes?"

"I don't want you to call me Mr. Dayton anymore. Call me Johnny." Johnny patted the butler on his shoulder, ignoring his look of surprise, and headed to his office to check his e-mail.

BRI-ING. BRI-ING.

Robin pushed away from her desk and headed to the phone. Knowing her mom would be calling back, she felt confident answering. "Hello?"

"Sweetie, I did what you asked," said her mother, who then proceeded to explain how the young mother had been listed in the Laramie directory, and had been very surprised to get a call from a stranger although she was very willing to talk.

"The OpticPower truck was three miles away from her ranch, the exact site where the cable had been severed," explained Robin's mother.

"But...why isn't that in the news?" asked Robin, thinking of the article forwarded to her by Suzanne. It had only said there was an alleged witness that the truck had been in the same vicinity of the cable, but gave no further specifics.

"Oh, sweetie, it's a sticky situation. Seems the teen-

age boy who saw the truck was riding a stolen motorbike. And worse, tested positive for drugs.''

"So he's not believable."

"That's the gist of it."

Robin listened, thinking how Johnny's younger
brother Frankie was like that—always getting into trouble. A bad seed, townsfolk called him, unlike his older
brother, Johnny.

Robin sat up, as though jolted. In her mind a picture
was forming...except one piece was missing.

"Mom," she said softly, "What was Johnny Dayton's
dad's name?"

Her mom paused. "I think...I think it was Paul.
Why?"

Robin's heart sank like a rock as she thought about
Johnny. One day wearing jeans and a T-shirt, like the
old Johnny. The next day, dressed in an expensive suit.
Taking the light-rail, then being picked up by a limo.
All a reflection of his conflicted soul, like a personality
torn in two. But saddest of all was the man who believed Agamemnon should have never returned home
because the man felt that way about himself.

Jpd stood for Jonathan Paul Dayton.

10

ROBIN'S FINGERS flew over the keyboard as she wrote the page of "talking points" for Johnny's—jpd's—speech. She was barely aware of the light rain against the window, the tap-tap-tapping as her fingers typed. Although this speech was about the young mother, the truth represented her own mother, as well. And what Robin couldn't say on the stand years ago, she was finally saying tonight through her written words.

It seemed as though she'd only been writing for a few minutes, but when Robin checked the clock, thirty minutes had passed. During that time, the rain had intensified. As she stared out the glass into the inky night, she thought how the truth, just like this storm, had been a long time coming.

And now she was ready to send the speech to Johnny, or jpd. Robin poised her finger over the send button and paused. Did Johnny know what OpticPower's communications department had asked her to write? "Stress that this is about a poor woman who wants to sue OpticPower for big bucks. Mention, at least twice, that the young mother has a history of debts. Underline that the only witness to the OpticPower truck severing the cable is some unreliable, drug-crazed kid who was joy-riding on a stolen motorbike."

Robin didn't know the ins and outs of corporate politics, but she guessed a man in Johnny's position relied heavily on his advisors to tell him the facts. But could Johnny easily blame an "unreliable" kid? Surely, it would hit too close to his own history and his brother Frankie.

Well, whatever his advisors told him—which was undoubtedly aligned with what the OpticPower communications department had told her to write—she hadn't put those things into the speech. Which meant she wouldn't be paid for what she'd written, but she didn't care. *I failed on the stand to tell the truth—but I can't fail now.*

She'd written about truth and accountability, and now it was up to Johnny if he'd use her—well, "Suzanne's"—speech or follow what his advisors wanted him to say.

She pressed the send button.

Robin clasped her hands together to stop their sudden trembling. *He'll view this speech as undermining him, damaging his company.* She got up and paced her living room, wringing her hands, feeling almost sick over what he'd certainly view as a betrayal. Then she stopped in front of the windows, watching rain flow in sheets down the glass. The water was pure, cleansing, bringing back Robin's sole intention as to why she wrote the speech as she did.

I only wanted to tell the truth, to protect that young mother.

If Johnny chose to use this speech, he'd be in direct opposition to what OpticPower's corporate spokesperson had already told the media—the same stuff they'd asked Robin to write. Maybe, as CEO, he wouldn't cross that line. But she had to take the chance that maybe he would.

That's why she'd ended the speech with a play on the word *stature.* First, it was part of OpticPower's slogan: Our Stature, Like Our Integrity, Rises Above All Others. But she'd given *stature* additional meaning by including a quote from Emily Dickinson:

We never know how high we are
Till we are called to rise
And then, if we are true to plan
Our statures touch the skies

She roamed around her living room, unable to wind down. She still wore her white rayon dress from work, and her hideous tennis shoes that squeaked as she roamed around her apartment. She thought about toying with one of her short stories or reading a book, but there was no way she'd be able to sit still. So she paced in circles as thoughts raced through her mind.

And thoughts of Johnny's integrity finally wound around to the fact that Johnny had spent hours the last few nights writing another woman, "Suzanne," while dating Robin! She stopped and stared at her reflection in the window. If people turned green with jealousy, her face was damn near chartreuse. "How dare he!"

The next moment, Robin laughed at herself. After all, she'd spent hours writing back to jpd, too. Then it hit her how perfect that two people who shared an intense physical attraction also discovered—well, accidentally discovered—they have an equally intense intellectual attraction as well. If this wasn't one of her mother's "signs from the universe," then she didn't know what was.

Feeling relieved, Robin stopped in front of her family photos and reflected on jpd's comment that he'd been "unable to protect his family." Robin had to hold her tears in check as she realized what Johnny had really meant. He'd been unable to protect his little brother or his father—it didn't take a genius to see that he was now driven to compensate by protecting his company and its employees.

"So that's what you meant by Agamemnon should never have returned home," she whispered to herself. Johnny couldn't return to Buena Vista, either. The townsfolk had never blamed Johnny for his brother's or father's problems, but she now realized how much Johnny blamed himself. And in that most profound sense, Johnny had spent his life feeling like a failure.

"You've Got Mail!" broke into her thoughts.

Robin stared at the laptop, took a fortifying breath, then crossed the room and sat down at the desk. She opened the e-mail—sure enough, a response from jpd@opticpower.net.

We're in a crisis. In the morning, I have to defend OpticPower and protect its employees...and despite my communications department coaching you on the speech's key talking points, you write a speech that feeds the media's monstrous portrayal of my company!

What are you thinking?

Robin's blood turned to ice. So *this* was Jonathan P. Dayton, CEO. Brusque, tough, dictatorial.

This is what had happened to Johnny. This was who he had become.

Yet, he hadn't told her to rewrite it. He'd just chewed her out. Maybe there was hope. Maybe his gut told him she was dead-on right—that this speech was more important than any legal-corporate-mumbo-jumbo crap he'd been told was true.

But she doubted it. Still, she couldn't back down. Fingers shaking, she wrote back:

Agamemnon had every right to return home. His only mistake was not making amends for the past.

Sometimes a man is stronger for not wearing a mask.

She knew that last line would rip into Johnny's soul. But it was true. It was time for him to give it up. He didn't need any kind of mask, whether it be as a CEO or like the African healer-protector mask he said he kept on his desk. He could just be Johnny, pure and simple, and be more powerful than any facade he thought he needed.

Tears clouded her eyes as she hit send and closed the monitor lid, which shut with a sharp click. She was through with e-mails, through with speech writing. Suzanne would freak when she saw this last bitter e-mail exchange between Robin and Johnny, but it was just as well. Robin would explain everything, tell the truth to Suzanne.

And while Robin was at it, she needed to own up to the truth herself. Tomorrow she'd call her family, tell them she'd dropped out of college, and that she wanted to come back home where she belonged.

TAP, TAP, TAP.

Robin awoke abruptly. Had she heard something? She strained to listen, but only heard the rain pelting against the window.

Tap, tap, tap.

There it was again. She raised up on one elbow, the blanket slipping off her shoulder. The adrenaline rush of writing that speech and responding to Johnny's accusatory e-mail had drained every last ounce of her energy. After all that, she'd had barely enough oomph to strip out of her clothes, lay out the sleeping bag, and toss a few blankets over herself before crashing into a deep sleep.

But now someone was tapping at her door? The building cat, Otto, when accidentally locked out of his own apartment, often scratched and whined at Robin's door in the wee hours, but this was definitely a tapping, not a scratching sound she heard.

She glanced at the clock—2:00 a.m.

Tap, tap, tap.

Her landlord? *It's raining harder—maybe someone's roof is leaking and he needs to check the other apartments.* Yawning, Robin wrapped herself in one of the blankets and shuffled to the front door. When she peered through the peephole, she thought at first the light had gone out in the hallway—all she saw was black.

Then the black lifted as the man raised his head and she recognized those unmistakable blue eyes.

Johnny.

His eyes burned with such pain, every muscle in her body tensed with urgency. She unbolted the door and threw it open.

Johnny stood hunched on the threshold wearing the clothes he'd had on this afternoon—the black leather jacket, white T-shirt and faded jeans—except the clothes, and the man, were drenched. She caught a scent of tannin from the wet leather, mixed with Johnny's scent—musky, masculine. Rainwater beaded his disheveled black hair. His blue eyes had darkened to gray, shielded by heavy, wet lashes. She'd seen different Johnnies in her life, but never the tormented man who stood before her now.

She wondered if somehow he'd put it all together—if he realized yet that she was the one who'd written the speech that tossed over what his advisors wanted him to say. Or that she'd lied about her identity. Was he here to chew her out, accuse her of deceit? She braced herself, ready for the brunt of his anger.

"I need you," he whispered hoarsely. He bent his head, as though too weary to say more. And for a fleeting moment, he looked like a warrior who'd lost the battle.

Instinctively, she opened her arms and pulled him into her embrace. He was chilled, his clothes soaked, but she didn't care. He needed her, needed *her*, and that's all that mattered. They silently clung to each other, a world unto themselves, for a long moment. Within her arms, she felt his tensed muscles, his ragged breaths. And she realized in her deepest heart that she was no longer just the girl who longed to go back home, but the woman whose love was Johnny's shelter.

Slowly, she eased from their embrace, drew him inside the apartment, and closed the door.

Wordlessly, she began undressing him. As she unzipped the soaked jacket, she guessed what had brought him to her tonight. He'd been lied to—at best, misled—by his advisors about what had happened in Wyoming. When he'd read a different version, Robin's take on the truth in the speech she'd written, Johnny's past and his present had finally collided. The man he used to be and the man he'd become were at war. He was torn, his soul a battlefield. And she prayed to God the Johnny she'd grown up with—the man with integrity and the unguarded heart—had won.

"Lean over," she said softly. He did, and she gently tugged his T-shirt over his head, vaguely aware her

blanket had dropped away. But she'd turned up the
heat when she came home, so she didn't feel uncomfortable. All that mattered was to take care of Johnny.
He'd been there for her during trying times—as a girl
afraid for success, as a woman struggling with failure.
And at this moment, she was here for him, heart and
soul.

After removing his shoes and pants, she ran to the
bathroom and grabbed the biggest towel she had. Returning with it, she rubbed him down, warming him.
Looking around, she realized she didn't have a damn
thing for him to put on, so she grabbed the blanket that
had fallen off her and wrapped it around him.

And only then, after she'd encased him in a large, tat-
tered pink blanket, did a slight smile crease his tired
face.

"I've never had a woman give me the blanket off her
back," he quipped.

And she wanted to say something back. Something
teasing and fun as an antidote to the cold, the hurt. And
she could have, probably, but his playful tone had a sad
undercurrent. She knew all too well what it was like to
always keep a lid on one's emotions, to not let people
know when turbulent thoughts and concerns churned
your very soul.

And then he surprised her.

"What happened to your mother?"

For a long moment, they stared into each other's eyes.
What had he heard? Considering everyone in Buena Vista
knew about the accident way back then, Johnny could

easily have run into someone who made a passing comment. Robin's memories of that event reached deep, into that dark part of her soul she tried to avoid. But if there was ever a time to reveal the truth, it was tonight. Tomorrow Johnny had to make a choice about his speech—maybe the truth about her mother would spur him to meet that young mother's truth.

"C-car accident." Damn, she was stuttering already. She took a deep breath, willing herself to say more...at least a few words more. She spoke slowly, picking her words as though tiptoeing through a minefield. "A kid ran...a st-st-op sign. Hit our c-car." She closed her eyes. *Just say the simple truth. No need to retell all the gory details.* Opening her eyes again, she finished, "Lies won." *In the same way your corporation is lying and wants to win.*

Johnny placed his fingers on her lips, as though knowing the agony of reliving the past. "And you were the only witness."

She nodded. If he didn't know more, he could certainly guess what happened. That she'd been unable to speak in her mom's defense. Tears welled in her eyes, for the past and for the future. It was all so complicated, and yet simple at the same time. What she hoped was that Johnny saw the parallel between her mother's story and that young mother's in Laramie.

She turned away, slightly, so he wouldn't see the emotion in her eyes. "Come to bed," she said softly, taking his hand and leading him to the opened sleeping bag. He lay down, still wrapped in the blanket, which he opened to invite her inside. She slid into the softness, relishing the cocoon of its warmth, and nestled against Johnny's strength.

Outside the window a passing gust of wind and rain rattled the window. Johnny tightened his hold around Robin and she closed her eyes, not wanting to worry anymore about the past or the future or what might or might not happen tomorrow. Right now, she just wanted to live in this moment of two people, stripped of their facades, sheltered in an embrace against the world.

Through the downy folds of the blanket, she reached for him, pleased when she touched the warmth of his muscled chest. She felt the pounding of his heart under her fingers and let her hand linger there, savoring the pulse of his life force and how it synchronized with the patter of the rain. Then she trailed her fingers across his body, gently touching his chest, his arms, his hands. For long minutes, she caressed and comforted him, showering him with love and gentleness—all the things the harsh world never gave to Jonathan P. Dayton.

"Robin," he whispered, "I love you."

Emotion surged through her as she smoothed back the still-damp tendrils of his hair. In all her dreams, she never thought she'd hear Johnny Dayton say those words to her. Outside, the clouds parted, allowing a stream of moonlight into the room. In that hazy light, she peered into his face. He looked so...relaxed. As though he'd relinquished his guard, let the mask slip.

She moved closer, inhaling his musky scent, and kissed him tenderly. This moment was too precious to speak, so she let her kiss say everything that lay in her heart. *I love you, Johnny Dayton. I've loved you forever...and will always love you.*

It was late. And she knew tomorrow he had to face a throng of reporters and their probing questions, a crowd of people incensed by the story of the young mother. Robin had thought it tough to stand at a podium at DU and give a few highlights on a homework assignment. She couldn't even fathom what Johnny had to face tomorrow morning. She brushed a second kiss on his cheek, a kiss to say good-night.

But his lips caught hers, covering her mouth, and she tasted his heat, his need. His hands found her breasts and he massaged her mounds, his fingers gently pulling and teasing her taut nipples. And when his erection stirred against her abdomen, her body awakened. She arched alongside him, rubbing herself against him, savoring the liquid heat of their bodies intertwining.

"Make love to me," he whispered, his voice thick with desire. He rolled onto his back, pulling her on top of him.

And she realized how this man who always had to be strong, had to be in control—who felt responsible for everyone from his family to his corporation—needed to be loved just for himself.

Lying prone on top of him, she stretched her arms until they encircled his neck and tangled her fingers into his dark, wet hair. Then, with a groan, she kissed him without restraint, branding her need on his mouth.

He returned her passion, their kisses growing frenzied as their tongues plundered and tasted each other.

Feeling his hardened arousal against her loins, she ached to feel him inside her. She hitched one leg alongside his hip, bracing the sole of her other foot on the floor. Then she hovered for a moment above him, sliding her hands down until they pressed against his chest for leverage.

Hovering over him, she slowly rubbed her wet mons back and forth over his swollen flesh. She'd slide forward, letting his member excite her nub, then slide back until he almost penetrated her. Back and forth she moved her body, enjoying the exquisite torture of teasing, being in control.

Or so she thought.

With a deep guttural groan, Johnny grasped her bottom and lowered her onto his hardened member, sinking her slowly down, down, letting his power fill her completely. Then, controlling her with his hands, he thrust and withdrew, over and over. Panting, whimpering, she dug her fingers into his chest, tightening her grip as his fierce lovemaking made her frantic with longing.

Lightning flashed outside and Johnny sucked in an appreciative breath at the sight of Robin, naked, astride him, her head thrown back, her breasts large, heaving. Lavender, mixed with her scent, soaked the air. She clutched at him with such a wild abandon, he knew he was seeing her true nature unleashed. No longer reserved, she opened herself to him, unashamed in her passion, the beautiful wild creature finally unveiled.

Then they were left in the dark again with rain smashing against the windows, as though the elements would break inside at any moment. And in the briefest of moments, it seemed as though the world stilled.

Then their passions exploded.

Fire seared deep in his gut as she screamed his name. Lightning flashed again, and in a moment of brilliant light, he saw her head thrown back, her body taut, clinging to him as though she couldn't contain the ecstasy. Then, wet, tight heat again enveloped him and he gritted his teeth, holding back, wanting to give her even more gratification. He thrust, deep, one last time, then cried out her name as he exploded within her.

She slumped on top of him, panting, the perspiration from her body slick against his skin. He brushed his fingers along her backside, returning the comfort she'd so sweetly given him earlier.

She shifted her weight, slipping to his side. They lay in each other's arms and looked out the window, watching the world through a curtain of rain. The twinkling stars blurred. The solid moon wavered. The world had changed, never to be the same.

IN THE WEE HOURS, Johnny woke up. The rain sprinkled against the glass—the worst of the storm was over. Johnny checked the clock—4:00 a.m. It was always like this before a work crisis—he'd have trouble sleeping. Often, he'd head to the kitchen and pour a glass of milk, make a sandwich and William would wander in, acting as though it were perfectly normal to be eating lunch in the wee hours of the morning.

Johnny looked at Robin, sound asleep. He smiled. She was the sweetest part of his life these days. Pure, untouched by the dirty venue of big business. That a woman like her even existed was a miracle in today's world. He felt the stirrings of need, again, but didn't want to wake her. Besides, the two of them were going to share more than just these past few days. For the first time in all his years, he knew he wanted to share the rest of his life with a woman.

With Robin.

Slipping from beneath the blanket, he walked quietly into the kitchen, grateful for the window over the kitchen sink because the moonlight gave him just enough light to see his way around. He gingerly opened the refrigerator door and checked its contents. Besides a half-eaten bag of salad, some eggs and what appeared to be a block of cheese that had seen better days, the rest of the fridge contained a multitude of plastic containers filled with everything from partially eaten pieces of cake to guacamole. Or he hoped that green stuff was guacamole.

And in the midst of this food fantasia, was a nice, simple, down-to-earth carton of milk.

At least she had fruit and vegetables hanging in that basket next to the fridge, but still, he'd have to talk to her about her eating habits sometime. He smiled to himself, realizing he felt protective of her.

Pouring the milk, he spied a small figurine nestled in the corner of the kitchen counter. Keeping the refrigerator door open for its light, he inspected the miniature cottage more closely. Then he remembered. These were the crafts Robin's mother made. He recalled how her mother took great pride molding and painting these little houses, often personalizing them as gifts for people. Ah, the simple, pure life of Buena Vista. He finished drinking the glass of milk and returned the carton to the fridge, relishing the jaunt down memory lane.

As he tiptoed back into the living room, a blinking green light across the room caught his eye. It appeared to be on Robin's desk. Odd, he hadn't noticed it earlier, but then, he'd been damn near out of his mind when he'd shown up here tonight. She'd taken him in, taken him to bed, and all he was aware of were her scents, their passion, his need to be accepted and loved by her.

He moved closer to the desk and recognized the light as emanating from the back of a laptop, its top closed. Funny, he hadn't noticed a computer at Robin's place before. The first night, her desk had been covered with coffee cups and books...and then Robin. He grinned at the memory. The second time when he'd been here, pacing, listening to her in the shower, he recalled stacks of papers and books on her desk, but he was so preoccupied with the Siren beckoning him, there could have been an elephant sitting on her desk and he probably wouldn't have noticed.

Maybe she'd borrowed this laptop from someone

and didn't realize she'd left it on. He'd take care of that quickly, then slip back under the blankets with her.

He lifted the lid. In the light from the screen, he scanned the keyboard for the power button when his gaze crossed the monitor.

He frowned.

There, open on the screen for him to see, was the message from Suzanne telling Johnny that Agamemnon could have gone home...

What the hell was Suzanne's e-mail message doing on Robin's computer?

Something inside him froze as he spied the listing of computer files displayed on the monitor behind the e-mail message: jpdspeech1.doc, jpdspeech2.doc, jpdspeech3.doc.

If he weren't a logical man, he might have grabbed at any illogical reason for his speech files, and this message from "Suzanne" to be on a computer in Robin's apartment. People made up excuses for others' behaviors—deluded themselves all the time—but not Johnny. He looked at his options, weighed the facts.

Rationally, there could be only one reason this computer, with these files, was in Robin's house.

Robin was Suzanne. Must be contracting through Suzanne—but Robin could have told him.

Betrayal had never tasted so sour. And bitter, he thought, while the irony of the situation sank in. The master spinner had been outspun, the lineman outdone. If he'd been less blinded by love—or whatever the hell he'd thought he'd felt earlier—he'd have put the clues together. How Suzanne and Robin both loved Emily Dickinson, how writing meant so much, how words had flowed eloquently from their fingers....

Why had Robin lied?

He gave his head a brusque shake, not wanting to figure it out. He dealt with power games every single day—it was a waste of energy to analyze people's motivations. Save that for the shrinks.

He crossed the room and put on his clothes, not giving a damn that they were damp and cold. All the better to wake him up to the real world. Nothing was pure. Or honest.

And when he shut the door behind him, he shut out this part of his life, too.

11

SUNSHINE GLISTENED on the window, matching Robin's mood. She glanced at the kitty clock. Nine-thirty! With a jolt, she looked around. No Johnny. She felt disappointed, but it made sense. She knew from Suzanne's message that the media conference was at 11:00 a.m. at the OpticPower main offices in downtown Denver. Johnny couldn't exactly tell her about this, of course, so he probably quietly got dressed and headed out early so he could put on the CEO suit, rehearse his talking points.

Anxiety cramped her stomach. What speech would he give? The Johnny who'd appeared on her doorstep last night had been tormented. And in her gut she knew why—he was struggling with the truth of what his company had, or hadn't, done. And how he could reconcile with the truth and still protect his employees as he had not done for his worthless old man or his beleaguered little brother Frankie.

He'd asked her about her mother, the accident. And when she told him, she saw his eyes shine with understanding. He had to have understood the point that sometimes a person's life can be rolled over by the machinery of lies and deceit—and that young mother in

Laramie was one of them. So would be Johnny, finally, if he listened to his coldhearted advisors.

Nine-thirty-five. Robin would have to hop on it if she wanted to shower, dress and catch a taxi so she could see Johnny's speech. Darn it all, anyway. She should have asked Johnny to wake her before he left, but that was the last thing on her mind when she'd drifted off to sleep in the wee hours....

Robin glanced over at the phone machine and saw the red light blinking. Maybe he'd called? She ran over and checked the message. A very pleasant woman, who identified herself as Shelia, said, "Robin, I'm calling on behalf of an anonymous benefactor who paid the Hudson Garage to release your vehicle. I made arrangements for your vehicle to be parked outside your residence, the car keys hidden underneath the floor mat."

Stunned, Robin ran to the windows next to the front door and peeked through the blinds. Sure enough, there sat her Jeep, "Em."

Shelia? Who's she? Robin crossed back to her phone machine and checked the caller ID next to it, which read "Private number." Robin glanced again at the clock. Nine-forty. Robin bet if she called the CEO's office at OpticPower, a "Shelia" would answer, but Robin didn't have time to investigate.

Then she noticed the laptop lid slightly open. Funny, she thought she'd closed it last night. She quickly shut it, vaguely surprised the computer was also powered off.

Too many things to think about, too little time. She

dismissed the thoughts and raced to the bathroom to get ready.

A HORN BLASTED as Robin swerved her Jeep into the right lane.

"Lady, where'd the hell'd you learn to drive? Indy 500?"

She glanced in her rearview mirror. Some preppie guy in a candy-apple-red convertible was shaking his fist at her. Robin smiled sweetly and waved before punching the gas. She had only a few minutes to get to 1800 California Street, the sixty-floor skyscraper that housed OpticPower's offices.

Minutes later, she squealed into a public parking lot, slammed to a stop in the first empty space, and tossed a ten-dollar bill at the parking attendant as she trotted toward the OpticPower building across the street. Ten bucks to park! Oh well, she'd skip lunch today. And tomorrow.

Robin raced across California Street, barely missing being hit by the light-rail, whose linked cars clattered rhythmically as it sped by. Outside the building a mass of people had gathered, at least a hundred. Reaching the edge of the group, Robin stopped and caught her breath. She'd never seen such chaos. Reporters, camera crews, people waving signs that said things like Might Doesn't Make Right! and OpticPower Severed the Truth!

She looked toward the steps that led to the building's glass doors. On the top few steps, about thirty feet from where she stood, a small group of suits congregated around a podium with a microphone. One of those suits was Johnny, who stood to the side of the podium, his head bent as he listened to some gentleman gesturing broadly as he explained something to Johnny.

From this distance, she couldn't see the look on Johnny's face. His clothes looked very different than what he'd worn last night when he appeared on her doorstep. Today he wore a charcoal suit, a powder-blue shirt and a striped tie. He appeared so polished, so in control, Robin had the eerie sense of watching some kind of robot, as though the man she knew had sunk below the surface.

Another member of the group, a tall thin man dressed as nattily as Johnny, stepped forward and spoke into the microphone. "Ladies and gentlemen, Mr. Jonathan Dayton, CEO of OpticPower Corporation."

A smattering of applause mixed with boos and taunts. Robin guessed the crowd consisted of loyal OpticPower employees and a contingent of angry Laramie residents.

"Good morning," Johnny said calmly, as though the chaos below him didn't exist. It stunned Robin to see him so detached. What had happened to the real man on her doorstep last night? She had a cold foreboding that that man wasn't here today.

The crowd grew so quiet waiting for Johnny to speak that Robin heard a child a few feet away cooing softly as he played with some trinket.

Johnny placed his hands on the podium and leaned

forward. "Recent allegations in the press have stated that OpticPower is responsible for severing a telephone cable outside Laramie, Wyoming, which in turn prevented a person from dialing 9-1-1. Today I want to state, unequivocally, that no OpticPower service truck was within a twenty-mile radius of that site...."

Ice flooded Robin's veins. He was parroting the company line, the words his communications department had dictated. In disbelief, she pressed through the crowd, wanting to be nearer. Wanting to see his face—did he really *believe* what he was saying?

"When you're a giant, like OpticPower, you're an easy target," he continued. Robin didn't like the sound of his voice. Authoritative. Arrogant. The people surrounding him reflected his attitude as they stood, their arms crossed, staring down their noses at the crowd below.

Robin squeezed through people to get closer. Those people up there had convinced Johnny to say these things. Had they lied, or only convinced him that this was the best way to protect his company? But it really didn't matter how he justified this madness. No explanation could stop the disappointment and fury pumping through her system.

Robin only stopped when she reached the bottom of the steps. She looked up at Johnny. Their eyes met. He paused. Then he looked around the crowd with a stoic air, as though he hadn't even seen her.

But he *had* seen her. Her stomach contracted to a tight ball. *He's ignoring me. Why?*

"There is a witness who alleges he saw an Optic-Power truck at the site of the severed cable." Johnny's jaw clenched as he paused again. "I ask you this. Would you believe a teenager on drugs? Would you believe a thief?"

"Yes!" Robin stood, rigid, not yet fully aware it had been she who'd yelled the answer. Suddenly, she felt as though she'd been dropped into a crack in time—one part of her felt as though she were again at her mother's trial, listening to lies. Another part of her was fully aware she was standing here in public, defending the truth for the young mother.

Her cheeks hot, Robin moved forward, breaking from the crowd. She again met Johnny's gaze, but this time he'd dropped his air of indifference. He looked strangely surprised.

That's when it hit her full force that she was speaking in front of a throng of people, including reporters and cameras. She hadn't thought this through, just reacted. Suddenly she felt hot, as though the sun burned brighter. She gulped a breath, her heart slamming against her ribs. She had to speak on behalf of that young mother. *Had* to. Robin had failed on the stand at her mother's trial, but she wouldn't fail now. This was Robin's second chance to speak up for the truth.

"You," she started. Damn it, she was shaking. She clenched her fists tight against her sides, willing herself to be strong. Taking a deep breath, she started again. "You want to protect your employees because you co-co-couldn't..." She swallowed, hard. "...pro-protect your family." Maybe she could will her body to stop shaking, but she'd never been able to control her stuttering. Maybe she should just turn and leave. Run away.

She blinked, fighting the raging panic within her. She'd run away too many times before. Run from the trial. Run from the podium at her university class. Run away from college...all because she stuttered.

If she ran away this time, she might as well keep running for the rest of her life.

One of Johnny's advisors, his eyes on Robin, leaned toward Johnny and whispered something in his ear. The man reminded Robin of Jill at the diner, probably putting Robin down, maybe suggesting ways Robin could be discreetly escorted away. Robin could imagine his whispered words. *Pathetic. Stutterer. She's making a fool of herself.*

Her anger escalated to a scalding fury. Damn it all to hell. It didn't matter what they said about her. Robin wouldn't let that young mother suffer the way her mother had.

"You have the power to help a woman and her son," Robin said loudly, pointing an accusing finger at Johnny. "You have the power to right a wrong." Within her swirl of emotions, she recalled her mother's words about the universe giving people second chances so they'd have another opportunity to make the right choice. Just as this was Robin's second chance, it was Johnny's, too. "You named your company 'Optic-Power'—so *give* it that power by telling the truth."

People began applauding. Microphones were stuck in Robin's face. "Do you know the young mother?" a pert auburn-haired reporter asked. "Did you speak to the teenager who saw the truck?" questioned another reporter.

Robin turned to the crowd, fury brewing through her, unafraid to speak the truth. She repeated the facts her mother had told her. "The young mother's name is Sandra Hayes. She's listed in the directory. Call *her*, ask for *her* side of the story. Sandra says the teenage boy, the witness, is a good kid who's done some bad things, but he's not a liar. OpticPower claims Sandra wants to sue them, but she doesn't want that. All she wants is the truth."

A weight lifted off Robin's heart as she started to walk through the people, who parted to give her passage. She'd carried the weight of her failure to help her mother all these years...and now it was gone.

Then she stopped. Turning, she looked back at the podium. "Tell the truth, Johnny. For Frankie."

Their gazes caught. For a fleeting moment, she swore a look of sadness shadowed Johnny's face. But when he remained silent, she turned and continued walking. She'd never look back again, no matter what the circumstances, because she was moving forward, living her own truth. And she was never, ever running away again.

JOHNNY WATCHED Robin walk away, ignoring the storm of reporters and cameras as the media surged up the steps. OpticPower's lawyer headed them off, coolly addressing their questions, while Johnny turned away and walked back to his office.

"Jonathan," called Christine, her high heels clicking against the cement as she scurried to catch up with him. "Great press conference."

"Bull." He didn't feel like playing the game anymore. Didn't want the sycophants and suck-ups who constantly told him what they thought he wanted to hear. He'd trade all their words for another one from Robin, but it was too late. The way she'd looked at him, he knew she wanted nothing to do with him ever again. And he'd never have the chance to tell her that despite her passionate defense of the young mother, his legal team had researched the situation, given Johnny the facts.

Christine's clicking shoes slowed momentarily. Jonathan hoped she'd gotten the hint, but no, the rapid click-click-click told him she'd caught up with him again.

"Jonathan, about Brad."

Jonathan stopped and turned to her. "Glad you brought the topic up, *again*," he said sharply. "I'm promoting him to vice president of Development."

Christine's mouth dropped open. "But…that's my position."

"It was. Until you wrote that memo to the board documenting 'facts' about Brad that were out-and-out lies." Something in Johnny's gut did a funny twist. Was it possible his legal team *lied* about that severed cable? Lied to protect the company?

"But—"

"Christine, you're fired. Pack up your desk."

He turned and walked away, wishing he'd handled this situation a long time ago. Wishing he'd done a lot of things better a long time ago.

He charged through the rotating glass doors into the building lobby, his mind reeling with thoughts, emotions. He felt furious Robin had deceived him by pretending to be Suzanne. At the same time, he felt awed at Robin's strength to stand there, surrounded by the swarm of media, and speak up for her beliefs. How the hell had she done that?

Her brother, Bud, had once told Johnny that when Robin got good and mad, she could "outtalk the best of 'em." Johnny smiled grimly to himself. She'd definitely been "good and mad" a few minutes ago—and damn eloquent. But that didn't mean she was right.

Last night, when he'd read "Suzanne's" speech, his first reaction had been anger. How dare this contract writer, who'd been given explicit instructions on what to write, turn around and write something totally different? It hadn't helped that he'd flipped on the news and seen that Laramie mother, talking about OpticPower's denial of its wrongdoing.

Torn, he'd again called his lawyer, who swore the evidence proved the mother wrong, that there had been no OpticPower trucks anywhere near the area of the severed cable. His lawyer had said the drugs the kid had taken were hallucinogenic so he'd had no sense of reality. "It's our word against a kid in la-la land," his lawyer had said.

After Johnny hung up, he'd felt conflicted inside. One part of him saw that young mother's face in his mind, so innocent, so scared for her son's life. But if his corporation was being wrongly accused, it hurt more than the company name. It hurt revenue. It hurt employees' paychecks. That's when he threw on his jacket and headed to Robin's. She was the one pure thing he could always turn to. She was like going home again.

Then, in the wee hours of this morning, when he'd read that e-mail and realized she had been masquerading as Suzanne, it was as though his focus sharpened. He suddenly saw the world again as it was. Harsh. Cunning. The face of innocence, like the faces of Robin and that young mother, didn't have a monopoly on the truth. Companies like his *were* deep pockets, ripe for the picking. And that's when he decided to be logical. To rely on his legal team's research and take the strong stance on behalf of OpticPower at the press conference.

Johnny took the express elevator to sixtieth floor. When the doors open, he marched toward his office.

"Check your e-mail," Shelia said quickly as he walked past her desk.

She knew his moods and could read a black one a mile away. He nodded briskly, entered his office and shut the door behind him. There'd be hundreds of e-mails, as there were every day. He knew Shelia would have combed through them all, marking which ones were critical, important and "could wait."

He sat behind his massive desk and flipped on his desk computer. As it hummed to life, he looked at the mask on his desk and something in him snapped. He'd spent his life trying to protect people. Maybe he was so caught up in the role of protector, he'd lost touch with what was truly worth protecting.

He grabbed the mask and tossed it into the trash can, then called out to Shelia to get Sandra Hayes on the phone for him. Then he changed his mind, and dialed Information for the young mother's number himself.

"HONEY BUN, time for you to get yourself home." Dottie, looking at herself in a compact mirror, applied red lipstick on her puckered lips. "Just 'cause it's your last night at work don't mean you do a full shift. Ain't that right, Al?"

Al flipped several burgers, the meat sizzling on the grill. "Whatever you say, Dottie Doll."

Smiling to herself, Robin rolled her eyes as she sliced another lemon. A week ago, if someone had told her that Al would turn into a lovestruck, "whatever you say, honey" kinda guy, she'd have wondered if they were talking about the same Al. *Amazing what love can do to a man.*

But as soon as she had that thought, her smiled faded. She grabbed another lemon, wanting to keep busy, not wanting to think about Johnny. But it was a futile wish. No matter how busy she kept herself, Johnny was on her mind. Last night, she'd thought she'd seen what love could do to Johnny. He'd needed her. Desired her. Told her he loved her.

Then, at the press conference, everything unraveled. It happened so quickly. One moment she was thrilled to see Johnny standing at the podium, and hopeful that the real Johnny would show up in his speech, and the next, stunned as he stated in that detached, professional tone that OpticPower was not at fault.

And then, she'd been even more stunned to realize *she* was talking! And talking. And talking. She still wasn't sure what she'd said, but she remembered people applauding, microphones in her face. She'd been furious...and she'd spoken fluently. She wished she didn't have to be one to be the other. She sliced the lemon in half, inhaling its tangy scent, wishing she could teleport herself back to a time before she'd left Buena Vista so all of this had never happened.

"Hell's bells," Al suddenly exclaimed. "Ain't that your boyfriend?"

Robin jerked her head toward the dining room. Johnny?

"The TV, honey bun," Dottie said, gesturing with a crimson fingernail to the small television Al kept next to the grill. He typically watched sports while he cooked, keeping the volume low, but tonight he had it on a local news station. Dottie took Robin's arm and guided her over to the TV. "Well, it's him, ain't it?" Dottie exclaimed. "Turn it up, Al, honey."

Al did as he was told.

Sure enough, there was Johnny speaking into a microphone.

"OpticPower has always stood behind its motto 'Our stature, like our integrity, is above all others,'" he began. "And tonight I want to apologize to Sandra Hayes on behalf of OpticPower because we haven't lived up to this motto."

Al slapped buns on top of the cooking hamburger meat. "Wearing a mighty fancy suit there," he grumbled, eyeing the TV. "He get your car fixed?"

"Don't talk while her boyfriend's talking," Dottie said. "Did he fix your car?" she whispered to Robin.

Robin nodded, feeling a swell of pride as Johnny explained how he'd personally contacted the mother, as well as the teenaged witness he had called a drugged-out thief, and now retracted his earlier statements regarding OpticPower not being responsible.

"He don't seem so bad," Dottie muttered, cocking her head as Johnny fielded some questions from reporters.

Al grunted, putting the burgers on plates. "Order up, Dottie."

She grabbed the plates, lining three along one arm, holding the fourth in her other hand. With a sassy little turn, she strolled out to the dining area, giving her walk a little extra oomph for Al's entertainment.

He chuckled, but stopped immediately when he looked at the TV again. "You still datin' him?"

Just like Dottie said, Al was nosier than Aunt Clarisse, whoever that was. "No," answered Robin. Until this moment, she hadn't really admitted it to herself. Probably because she'd been so busy ever since she got home after the press conference this morning. She'd given her work and her landlord notice, made plans for her brother to drive out and help her pack. Tonight the two of them were driving back to Buena Vista.

But this time she wasn't running away, she was moving toward something. She was returning home, where she belonged.

She watched Johnny on TV, fielding questions with grace and candor, admitting OpticPower had been at fault, but despite this change of events, she knew it would never work for the two of them. Her world and Johnny's had crossed because they needed to help each other get back on their right paths. Two totally different paths. Johnny belonged to a bigger world, one of big business and high stakes. Robin belonged to a smaller world, one filled with family, friends and the possibility of making a dream or two come true.

On the TV, Johnny held up his hands to make a final statement. "Before I go, I'd like to quote from a great poet, Emily Dickinson, the favorite of a friend of mine. 'We never know how high we are/Till we are called to rise/And then if we are true to plan/Our statures touch the skies.'" He paused, looking intently into the camera. "Thank you."

And for a moment, Robin wondered if that "thank you" was for her, just as, years ago, she stood at a podium and said a "thank you" to him.

Robin rigidly held her tears in check as she removed

her apron. It was time to go. She was ready to leave Davey's Diner, leave Denver, leave perhaps the most wonderful moments of her life, but it was time for her, too, to be true to her plan.

12

AN HOUR LATER, Robin looked around her empty apartment. Her brother, Bud, had done a great job packing up her things while she was at work, although she owned so little in the world, it probably took him all of an hour to cart some furniture and pack a few boxes. They were almost ready to start the drive home to Buena Vista. Bud was rearranging furniture and boxes in the trailer while Robin did a last check of her place and changed into some sweats for the drive home.

She looked around her living room, part of her wishing Johnny would materialize out of the woodwork and take her into his arms while another part of her reminded herself again that it'd never work. *Wouldn't her mother be proud of that little self-realization!* Robin not succumbing to an overdramatization of events, just a logical assessment that she and Johnny would never mix. Like eggplant and chocolate. Like F. Scott Fitzgerald and Emily Dickinson.

Like, get real. If she and Johnny had had their acts together, they could've been the hottest thing since Haley's Comet. But she could get real, she could accept that she and Johnny would never mix, but that didn't stop her heart from breaking. Spasms of grief shook her as she thought how, like Haley's Comet, her and Johnny's love had soared, flamed, reached heights she'd never dreamed possible. Then they'd crashed and burned.

Rolling back her shoulders, Robin dashed her tears and forced herself to finish, to wrap up this part of her life and move on. At least Johnny had made his amends to the young mother, and for that she was glad. He'd taken a second chance and made a wrong, right. Someone, or something, had gotten to him, inspired him to delve into the facts himself, to correct his mistake and do the right thing.

But that someone hadn't been Robin. Johnny hadn't believed Robin when she pleaded with him to rethink his stance...and their worlds had irrevocably ripped apart at that moment.

All that remained in the room were Mick in his cage and the laptop, which sat in a far corner. Earlier, Robin had called Bud from Davey's Diner and asked him to phone Suzanne Doyle and get directions to her house so they could drop off the computer on their drive home.

Robin crossed to the laptop, sat cross-legged on the floor and turned the computer on, telling herself she should delete the conversational e-mails between her and Johnny. *Not reread them, delete them.* She smiled sadly to herself, knowing the last thing she needed tonight was a trip down memory lane. She bit her lip. Another trip down memory lane, down that lane that had persisted in her dreams since Johnny had sat front-row-center in the school auditorium so she could say a sim-

ple thank you...another trip would kill her. Just being in
this room, recalling the times she and Johnny had made
love was a painful enough memory. Honest to God, she
could still smell his scent. That intoxicating mix of mas-
culinity and musk that shot straight to her head, made
her crazy.

"You've Got Mail!"

Robin blinked. Had to be an e-mail for the *real* Suzanne, not for Robin. She opened the e-mail program.
There was a message from jpd@opticpower.net with
the subject line "Robin, please read this."

Alarms clanged within her.

Robin, please read this?

How did he know Robin had access to Suzanne's ac-
count? Had he known all along that it was Robin, not
Suzanne, writing to him, drafting those speeches? *Impossible.* Suzanne would have had to tell OpticPower's
communications department or tell Johnny personally,
and neither scenario made sense. Suzanne's legal agree-
ment with OpticPower was for all contracting work to
be billed under Suzanne's name.

An image flashed through Robin's mind. This morning, right before she'd jumped in the shower, she noticed the laptop monitor lid slightly open. But thinking
back, after the angry e-mail exchange with jpd the night
before, Robin distinctly recalled clicking the lid closed.

A dreadful clarity gripped her. *Johnny read the messages, realized I'm "Suzanne."* Her heart sank, realizing
how betrayed he would have felt. But when did he have
access to this laptop? Had to be in the middle of the

night, maybe early this morning, while she was still asleep. She groaned, wishing she'd had the good sense to just turn off the damn computer last night, not simply close the lid.

No wonder he seemed distant, cold even, when he saw me in the crowd this morning before his speech. Taking a deep breath to steel herself, she opened Johnny's e-mail message.

Dearest Robin,
Last night, I accidentally discovered you were writing as Suzanne. At first I felt duped because I viewed you as the purest, most honest thing that has ever come into my life. I felt that if you could deceive me, anyone could deceive me.
I was so wrong.
I gave a second news conference this evening. Afterward I called your work. They told me you're moving back home. I want to leave you with this goodbye message.
There are the days when birds come back
A very few—a bird or two—
To take a backward look.

Robin read and reread the verse. He'd selected it from one of her favorite Emily Dickinson's poems, and she pondered if a bird or two meant she or Johnny—or both of them—were "coming back." She finally decided it didn't matter. Maybe all he wanted her to understand was that he valued the "backward look"—that he hoped she would always reflect lovingly on what they'd shared.

She started to write back, but changed her mind. In a way, they'd said it all.

Minutes later, dressed in her sweats—carrying Mick's cage in one hand, the laptop in the other—Robin wandered through the apartment, ensuring nothing was left behind. She paused in the kitchen and admired the recipes and pictures of food she'd decoupaged on the cabinet doors. What had Suzanne said Robin's kitchen reminded her of? Provence? *For a small-town girl, I brought a bit of the south of France to the big city of Denver.* Coddling that thought, Robin headed to the living room.

There, she stood in front of the windows for the last time. During these past months, she'd often look at the sky and wondered if her mother or brother were sharing the same view.

And in the future, I'll look up at the sky in Buena Vista and wonder if Johnny shares the same view as well. And if he remembers a Robin who flew away, but often takes a backward look, wondering how her Johnny is.

A DAVE MATTHEWS tune was cranking on the radio. Robin danced and strutted to the beat as she moved along her shelf of books, looking for a particular reference tome that contained leadership quotes. Something about vision, strategy or leadership would be the perfect pièce de résistance on an article she'd been finishing for a local politician. Scanning book titles, Robin sang along with the music, feeling the sultry vibes of the saxophone while she harmonized with the male singer's gravelly voice.

She'd opened her business, Lee Writing Services, five months ago in Buena Vista, starting out doing contract copyediting along with writing proposals and miscellaneous documentation. But as word spread, Robin added on new writing jobs—everything from speeches to articles to book reviews for the local newspaper. The latter had been especially rewarding as that had been her goal when she'd applied to college—to be a book reviewer—she just never dreamed she'd end up doing it in her own hometown. Nor did she dream she'd be finishing her college Lit degree from her hometown, but now she would thanks to Suzanne e-mailing Robin about a DU-affiliated Internet college program. Plus, Suzanne had recently e-mailed Robin with other freelance job leads, which boosted her income.

Robin still lived at home with her mother, but if Lee Writing Services kept on this upward swing, she'd soon have her own little place. Well, hers and Mick's place.

The lead singer's voice took off on a different tangent. He didn't sound so gravelly, either. Robin paused, bobbed her head to the beat, then struck a new chord as she harmonized heartily with the switch in the tempo. She sang more these days. Talked more, too, thanks to the speech therapy she started after moving back home.

She wasn't sure at what point she realized it was an ad playing on the radio—a man pitching insurance coverage—not music playing.

If that was true, who was she harmonizing with? She stopped singing and turned around.

Johnny slouched against the open door of her business, his eyes glistening with a look that made her insides cave in. Aimlessly, she pawed at the radio knob and turned down the volume. Her heart surged painfully against her rib cage as she and Johnny stared at each other for what seemed forever.

His face looked relaxed, the way it had been that late, stormy night they'd made love to the rain and lightning. A dizzying current raced through her as she remembered their passion.

She managed to wrench her gaze from his dangerously blue eyes and peruse the rest of him. He was dressed again like the old Johnny—faded jeans, T-shirt, jacket—and yet he looked different. She glanced back at his face. That's where the difference lay. He was not only relaxed, but he had that easygoing, devil-may-care grin she remembered from years ago. It was like looking again at the old Johnny, the guy who'd stolen her heart so many years ago...the guy who still had her heart.

"You look great." His husky voice sent tremors through her.

"You, too."

His eyes flashed surprise at her quick response. She smiled. "I've been taking speech therapy," she announced proudly, raising her chin a notch.

He cocked an eyebrow. "Good. For a moment, I was worried you were angry with me."

"Angry?" A laugh erupted from her as she caught his meaning. "You have a wicked sense of humor."

He didn't say anything, just shot her such a deliciously sinful look, she had trouble just breathing in and out for a few moments.

"So," she finally said, having no idea what to say next. "Haven't seen you in months." Six months, two weeks, one day to be exact.

"It's been a few."

Damn him, anyway.

"Six, I believe."

The man was superior to the rest of the race. "Yes, I think it's been about that," she said softly, fighting a smile of immense satisfaction that he'd remembered. "So," she began again, shuffling one foot slowly back and forth as another tune played quietly on the radio. She looked over his shoulder and saw a shiny SUV with a moving-company trailer in tow, parked in front of her office building. "Is that yours?" she blurted.

He glanced over his shoulder, then back to her. "Yeah."

Yeah? The guy drops out of the sky, turns her world upside down, then says, *yeah,* he's moving somewhere? Did he have any idea how much her heart *still* ached just at the mere thought of him? She crossed her arms under her breasts and paced a few feet before stopping short and glaring at him. "So, do you tell me what's up or do we play twenty questions?"

He looked momentarily taken aback. "Is speech therapy also teaching you to be sassy as hell?"

"No, I've always been sassy, just nobody knew."

He grinned. That deliciously wicked grin that sent sparks of heat skittering across her skin. "Well, I can see that it's bigger than a bread box," she prodded. When he continued staring at her, she motioned with a shaky hand toward the SUV so he'd understood what "it" meant. She quickly folded her arms again, but it was too late. He'd seen the effect he was having on her. But she would have to be a lifeless, bloodless statue to not feel all the emotions that surged through her. Just looking at him brought back sizzling images of their naked bodies, the sweet taste of his kiss, the liquid heat of his skin against hers....

He looked at her so intensely, she swore he'd just read every hot thought searing through her brain.

"It's bigger than a bread box because it holds everything I own. I've left the big city, returned to Buena Vista—"

Returned? "For good?" She blinked, realizing she'd cut him off but unable to stop herself. How many times had she fantasized seeing Johnny again on the streets of their hometown. Fantasized about their talking, spending time together and maybe, just maybe there'd be the opportunity for a second chance.... But she always stopped there, reminding herself that such dreams were just salves for her wounded heart. "You're here to stay?" *Why would he leave the big city, big business?* When he nodded, she thought for a moment then frowned. "For your health?" When he shot her a confused look, she explained quietly, "The heart murmur."

Johnny hadn't known what he'd find when he walked into Lee Writing Services. Robin's mother hadn't seemed all that excited to divulge the whereabouts of her daughter's business, which left Johnny wondering if one, maybe Robin's mother didn't want her to get involved again with Johnny Dayton, who, despite all his business successes, was still the tough kid from the wrong side of town, or two, whether Robin's old boyfriend had resurfaced, or worse yet, three, she'd gotten herself hitched to some other lucky guy.

But looking at Robin now, with her pink cheeks, her blond hair pulled on top of her head in a lovely curly confection, she was again his Gibson Girl. All alabaster and pink...but also independent and strong. His Gibson Girl had grown into a woman who controlled her life, her destiny.

"Your heart murmur?" she repeated, concern darkening her eyes.

"Yes," he whispered, responding to her question. "I returned to help my heart murmur...." He looked around the room, seeing if there were any photos or other indications that another man had replaced him. There was a photo of Robin's family and a picture of Robin and a girlfriend smiling happily. But no pictures of men. "And fortunately," Johnny said, returning his gaze to Robin, "it's murmuring just fine."

He stepped closer. "And I returned to build a teen center, the kind of place Frankie would have benefited from. In fact, Frankie and I are in contact again—I'm trying to convince him to move back, be a counselor for the kids." Johnny skipped the part about visiting his dad's grave again, too. After all these years, he'd finally made his peace with his father.

"Wow," Robin breathed. "You're planning a lot...."

He stepped closer, catching a familiar whiff of that lavender scent that did crazy things to his insides. "I had another plan, too. One involving your mother."

"My mom?"

"I know some store chains that would pay good money for those miniature houses she makes. It's just a thought...."

A look of appreciation spread across Robin's face. "We, I mean, you can broach the subject with her. Maybe drop by the house sometime...."

"I'd like to do that because I have another proposal." He was so near, he could touch her. Ached to touch her.

She raised her eyebrows in a question.

"The teen center could use a good writer. Someone who can design a marketing campaign, write a newsletter, those sort of things." The nearness of her made his entire damn body hurt. She wore a pretty pink dress, and he could just imagine what lay beneath the prim, buttoned-up outfit.

She licked her lips. "Would that be a temporary project...or long term?"

"Depends upon what the lady wants," he answered huskily. "Which I have no doubt she'll say because she has a growing reputation for speaking her mind."

Robin's smile grew until it brightened her whole face. "Considering the lady is no longer tongue-tied, the first thing she wants to say is, how come you're standing so close and not taking advantage of her?''

That did it. Johnny tunneled his fingers into her silky hair and stamped his mouth on hers, kissing her until he felt her go hot and soft. Then he pulled his head free, trailed his fingers down her cheek, and looked into her sparkling green eyes...the greenest he'd ever seen. The kind of fervent green where lush and wild dreams grew.

''The lady hasn't told you everything she wants,'' Robin said breathlessly, holding his gaze.

Johnny pulled her tight against him and murmured, ''Whatever the lady wants, the lady gets...for as long as she'll have me.''

Needing no more encouragement, Robin whispered what she desired, for the rest of her life, into her Johnny's ear.

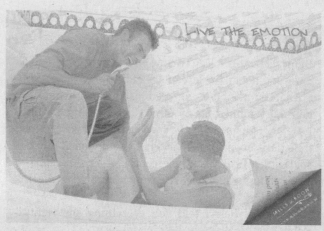
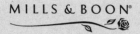

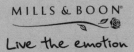

FREE!

2 Books

and a surprise gift!

We would like to take this opportunity to thank you for reading this Mills & Boon® book by offering you the chance to take TWO more specially selected titles from the Sensual Romance™ series absolutely FREE! We're also making this offer to introduce you to the benefits of the Reader Service™—

★ FREE home delivery
★ FREE gifts and competitions
★ FREE monthly Newsletter
★ Books available before they're in the shops
★ Exclusive Reader Service discount

Accepting these FREE books and gift places you under no obligation to buy; you may cancel at any time, even after receiving your free shipment. Simply complete your details below and return the entire page to the address below. *You don't even need a stamp!*

YES! Please send me 2 free Sensual Romance books and a surprise gift. I understand that unless you hear from me, I will receive 4 superb new titles every month for just £2.60 each, postage and packing free. I am under no obligation to purchase any books and may cancel my subscription at any time. The free books and gift will be mine to keep in any case.

T3ZEB

Ms/Mrs/Miss/Mr ....Initials ....
BLOCK CAPITALS PLEASE

Surname ....

Address ....

....

....Postcode ....

Send this whole page to:
UK: The Reader Service, FREEPOST CN81, Croydon, CR9 3WZ
EIRE: The Reader Service, PO Box 4546, Kilcock, County Kildare (stamp required)

Offer not valid to current Reader Service subscribers to this series. We reserve the right to refuse an application and applicants must be aged 18 years or over. Only one application per household. Terms and prices subject to change without notice. Offer expires 28th November 2003. As a result of this application, you may receive offers from Harlequin Mills & Boon and other carefully selected companies. If you would prefer not to share in this opportunity please write to The Data Manager at the address above.

Mills & Boon® is a registered trademark owned by Harlequin Mills & Boon Limited.
Sensual Romance™ is being used as a trademark.